Robert Grant

Jack in the bush

Or a summer on a salmon river

Robert Grant

Jack in the bush
Or a summer on a salmon river

ISBN/EAN: 9783743303188

Manufactured in Europe, USA, Canada, Australia, Japa

Cover: Foto ©Andreas Hilbeck / pixelio.de

Manufactured and distributed by brebook publishing software
(www.brebook.com)

Robert Grant

Jack in the bush

MAN DARTED FORWARD WITH UPLIFTED ARM, AND STRUCK WITH
ALL HIS MIGHT. — P. 270.

JACK IN THE BUSH

OR

A SUMMER ON A SALMON RIVER

BY

ROBERT GRANT

AUTHOR OF "JACK HALL," " FACE TO FACE," "THE CONFESSIONS
OF A FRIVOLOUS GIRL," ETC.

———

BOSTON
JORDAN, MARSH & COMPANY
1888

RAND AVERY COMPANY,

ELECTROTYPERS AND PRINTERS,

BOSTON.

CONTENTS.

CHAPTER VII.

CHAPTER VIII.

CHAPTER IX.

JACK IN THE BUSH.

CHAPTER I.

OFF TO THE WOODS.

If you will look at the map, and observe the course of the St. Lawrence River, you will see that, after passing the City of Quebec, as it grows broader it gradually bends to the east; and that where it empties into the gulf of the same name, the whole right-hand coast falls away, describing a curve which does not cease until it unites with the eastern shore line of the Dominion. The tongue of land thus formed, lying between the St. Lawrence on the northwest, and the Bay of Chaleur on the southeast, and shaped not unlike the end of a hockey, is a part of the Province of Quebec, and is, save for the occasional fishing villages on the coast, an unsettled tract of country, almost uninhabited, and covered with forests, among which perpetual snow reigns from October until June.

Yet, uninviting as it seems from the standpoint of civilization, the sportsman can find in this domain many of the wild creatures, both birds and fish, which avoid the neighborhood of man. Throughout it and the northern portion of New Brunswick, the Canadian province adjoining on the south, bears and caribou and many varieties of small game are abundant. But that which distinguishes the region more especially is the presence of the salmon. This splendid fish makes its summer home in the rivers which empty themselves along the curving shore from the banks of the St. Lawrence to the Straits of Northumberland. Apart from the attractions of sport, there is magnificent scenery in these Canadian woods, — pine-clad mountains, cascades and stretches of foaming water adapted to try the skill of canoe-men; and, to interest one who sails along the coast in search of a harbor, bold headlands and tall precipices, against which the sea dashes itself viciously, even when smiling.

Mr. John Holt, — a college graduate of thirty-five, — in looking out for a site for his summer school, happened to apply to his old friend and chum Randolph Russell, whose splendid physique and bronzed skin were in keeping with the reputation he had won as a hunter of big game in many lands.

"I wish," Mr. Holt said, "to find some place where I can take half a dozen boys to spend the summer, with a prospect of bracing air and good sport. I have a plan for a summer school."

"A school in summer!" ejaculated Colonel Russell. "Don't they get study enough during the rest of the year?"

"I don't wonder you are not prepossessed in its favor at first blush," answered his friend. "Neither were the boys until it was explained that the term 'school' in this case did not imply lessons in the usual sense. I've. had the idea for some time that there are a great many parents at a loss how to provide their sons during the holidays with healthful occupation. If one were going to Europe or to some fashionable watering-place, or were obliged to spend the summer in town, or a child were delicate and needed some invigorating change, it seemed to me as though it would certainly be a boon to have a young man like myself come and say, 'Let me take your boy for eight weeks into the back-woods. He will have pleasant companions, the best of air, simple food, and whatever discipline he needs. I will bring him back to you brown as a berry, and in excellent condition to resume his studies.' Accordingly I acted upon my theory, with the result that I have six pupils engaged for the season, and could have more were I willing to undertake the responsibility of a large number. Now, I've come to you to tell me where to go to."

"Quite right. I must consider," said the Colonel. "Six boys together in the woods! You will have your hands full, my dear fellow."

"Perhaps; but I shall enjoy the experience. I trust we shall all enjoy it, and if I can hit on the right spot I feel sure we shall have a capital time. The difficulty is to find a camping-ground which combines fresh air and beautiful surroundings with sport. I can think of half a dozen places where we should have beautiful scenery

and plenty of ozone, but the boys would come
home next to empty-handed in the way of fish
and birds. I don't want to go to a place which is
fished out and shot out."

"Precisely, and it is not very easy to find nowadays a place such as you have in view. But I
happen to know of an excellent one if you don't
object to going some distance from home."

"What do you mean by 'some distance,' —
Central Africa or the jungles of India?"

"If you like; but I had especially in mind a
salmon river in the wilds of Canada."

"A salmon river! That sounds well."

"I happen to be the lessee of the fishing-rights
on one of the rivers in the county of Gaspé, in
the far northeastern corner of the Province of
Quebec," continued the Colonel, "and I should be
very glad to have you and the six boys enjoy
them with me this summer. It takes about three
nights and three days to get there; but I can
promise you fine sport unless there is an unusually
poor run of fish."

"The very thing, I should say. But are you
not rashly flying in the face of Providence in

making such a proposal? As you said yourself just now, think of six boys together in the woods! You will not have a moment's peace."

"I guess I can stand them if you can."

"You forget that it is my profession to stand them," answered Mr. Holt.

"And you forget that I have faced nearly every variety of formidable creature the world over, — lions, tigers, orang-outangs, and what not."

"I give in, then; for I can guarantee, I think, that my boys are not so formidable as all that. Indeed, I believe them to be very good fellows. Before accepting unequivocally, however, I should like to make the condition that we rough it a little. I imagine that an old sportsman like yourself does not surround himself with superfluous assistants, but I should like to have as few as it is possible to get along with. My idea is that the boys should do their own tent-building and rowing and cooking, with a woodsman or two to show them how."

"With all my heart," said the Colonel, puffing at his pipe by way of vigorous approbation of this sentiment. "The river is a bit steep in spots, but if you're ready to take hold and do some poling yourself we ought to get on capitally with the help only of William Patterson, who looks after my traps at Gaspé Basin, and his son Jimmy."

"I'm game for any amount of work," said Mr. Holt.

"I'll write to-morrow and tell William that we are coming. Who are your boys, by the way?"

"There's Jack Hall from Boston, whom you know already, I think, and a friend of his who rejoices in the nickname of 'Dubsy' Perkins, though he was christened ·Samuel. Then there's a St. Louis lad named Haseltine who is at the same boarding-school as Jack, two New Yorkers Max and Joe Fearing, and Tom Binney from Philadelphia, — a very manly appearing set, take them all together, though my knowledge of them is necessarily superficial. The younger Fearing is about fourteen, and the others not far from sixteen."

"Well, we'll make men of them," said the Colonel.

"If I had known I was to have your co-operation, my dear Randolph, I should have charged a larger tuition fee. When my pupils hear that they are to go into camp with one who has killed bears and tigers in hand-to-hand combat, the expedition will become very popular."

As a result of this conversation, the two gentlemen and the six boys, whose names you have been told, set out one evening in the latter part of June for Gaspé Basin, the village close to which Colonel Russell's river emptied into the sea. A night in a sleeping-car brought them to Montreal. There they spent the day, and in the afternoon they took the boat down the St. Lawrence as far as Quebec, where the boys were thrilled at the approach in the early morning to the magnificent heights towering above the river, at the base of which the city is built, — one of the grand views of the world. There was no time, however, to spend in roaming about the picturesque old place, for the train was in waiting; and away they went flying farther north, following the curving right bank of the river, past French Canadian towns, each consisting of a bevy of cottages nestled about a vast church with a tall spire, the tin covering of which glistened in the sunshine. In the afternoon the train branched off to the east, and immediately they were travelling through what had been but a few years before virgin wilds, and where even now the engine was the sole explorer. At sunset time the scenery became more attractive. Mountains appeared, and through the windows of the cars they looked down on a spirited river winding its way along, here calmly, and at the next glimpse alive with foaming rapids.

"The Metapedia," said the Colonel. "It and the Restigouche, with which it unites a few miles below, are two of the finest salmon rivers in Canada."

Presently they came in sight of a canoe with three men in it, the middle one of whom was fishing, while the two others held the boat steady with long poles.

"See, see," Colonel Russell cried, "he has a fish on."

"A salmon?" ejaculated several of the boys.

"Certainly. A lively one, too, by the way he acts."

Sure enough, the angler's rod was bent at a

considerable angle, and the line seemed to be running out at an exceedingly lively pace. All of a sudden, just as they were abreast of the canoe, something jumped out of the water and flashed for a moment nearly a hundred yards ahead.

"Did you see him jump?" cried the Colonel. "Ah, he has lost him!"

"Where? how?" exclaimed the boys excitedly; but the canoe was no longer in sight.

"The salmon leaped out of water, as they often will; and I could tell by the way the line slackened that he was off. He must have broken the hook, or fallen on the casting-line and snapped it," the Colonel explained. "Either is a very frequent occurrence."

An hour later they reached Campbellton, a small railroad town at the western extremity of the Bay of Chaleur, and on the dividing line between the provinces of New Brunswick and Quebec, where they passed the night; and early in the morning they went on board the propeller "Admiral," which plies between Campbellton and Gaspé Basin, — a sixteen-hour trip in average summer weather, with allowance for half a dozen

stops at the fishing-villages along the coast. It
was a beautiful day, and the boys were at first
absorbed in looking out for white porpoises,
which are to be seen in large schools through
the Bay of Chaleur; but, though they failed to
catch sight of any, they speedily forgot their
disappointment in listening to the account which
the Colonel gave them of the hard existence led
by the fishermen, and the wives and daughters
of the fishermen, who inhabit the grand but iron
shore along which the steamer passed. Long
years before, he said, merchants from the far
distant island of Jersey had erected hereabouts
a series of establishments for the catching and
cure of cod, herring, and mackerel, affording a
pitiful livelihood to the natives, upon whom
Nature smiles but for a brief spell in summer,
and who for the greater part of the year are shut
out from intercourse with the rest of the world.
Nevertheless, the villages of Port Daniel, Pabos,
and Paspebiac, at which the " Admiral " stopped
for a few moments, looked attractive in the balmy
June sunshine, with their big storehouses outlined
against the green hills.

"Well, boys," said Mr. Holt, looking at his watch, "we ought to be at Gaspé in about four hours; and I shall take this opportunity, when we are all quietly seated together, to make you a little address. As you know, your parents have intrusted you to me with the wish that you should be brought back refreshed for another year's work at school. I expect that our life in camp will strengthen your muscles, teach you to wait upon yourselves, and to be energetic and courageous. If it doesn't, I shall be disappointed. I know something about camping out myself, and our friend here, Colonel Randolph Russell, knows all that is worth knowing on the subject: so it will be any boy's own fault who does not return at the end of the summer a thorough back-woodsman. But though I hope you will all enjoy yourselves mightily," he continued, "you mustn't suppose that every thing will be easy as rolling off a log, as my old guide used to say. Although there will be no lessons in the ordinary sense of the word, except an occasional lecture from me or Colonel Russell on the natural history, for instance, of the fish and birds that may be killed by you, I shall regard you all as scholars to the extent that I shall expect you to keep up to the mark in whatever you undertake, whether it be angling or poling or gunning or cooking. For, boys, we shall have to cut down trees, and build our own fires, and cook our own dinners, and propel our own canoes. That may sound like fun, and I have no doubt it will be fine fun; but there will be times, you may depend upon it, when you will feel that you'd rather be doing this, that, or the other than the especial thing which it is your turn to do, and at those times, Jack and Tom and Max and Joe and Frank and Sam, you must show yourselves to be the manly, unselfish boys I believe you to be. That's all I have to say at present."

The silence which followed was broken at length by Colonel Russell's remarking, "I've got something to show you, boys;" after which he arose, and, going below, reappeared presently with a fine double-barrelled shot-gun.

"There," he said, "since this is a school, I am going to put up a prize. The boy who makes the best record shall have this."

A murmur of satisfaction ran through the group.

"My eye!" ejaculated Haseltine.

"Do you mean the boy who catches the most fish?" asked Jack Hall eagerly.

"Or who shoots a bear?" said Tom Binney.

"Or the boy who cooks best?" said Dubsy Perkins.

The Colonel pursed up his lips and looked wise. "What I said was the boy who makes the best record," he remarked slowly. "That may be the boy who catches the most fish, or it may be the boy who shoots a bear, or the one who cooks the best, and it may be none of them. There are lots of things that go to make up a good record as a sportsman. One must show nerve and grit and prudence and agility and common-sense and handiness and a great many other qualities; and all I can say is, that the boy in this party who exhibits most of them during the time we are in the woods together is to have this gun, and it may be, too, he will not have shot or caught a single thing. One may be unlucky and yet a far better sportsman at bottom than a fellow who goes out walking and stumbles on a moose, or who runs across fish in the rising mood and fills his canoe. Give me the angler who can make fish rise when they don't want to. Hulloa," he added, breaking off, " there's the Percé Rock."

Every one followed the direction of his finger. The steamer was approaching an enormous picturesque crag towering above the sea at a short distance from the shore, remarkable from the fact that there was an archway through it large enough to afford a passage to a moderate sized skiff without peril to sail or spar.

"It has been gradually eaten through by the action of the waves and weather on the stone," said the Colonel. "Is it not interesting? Do you see those dark specks which cover the top? They are all birds. When you get a little nearer, you shall see something curious."

Thereupon he went forward and said a few words to the captain, and ten minutes later, when the " Admiral " was but a short distance from the rock, boom! rang the noise of a cannon at the steamer's bow.

Instantly the whole army of birds, of which there were hundreds, arose in a white flapping mass and soared above their eyrie with wild screeches. The air seemed alive with them.

"What are they?" asked one of the boys.

"Gulls, gannets, and cormorants chiefly, answered the Colonel. "Birds that live on fish. That broad, flat top is a famous place for their nests, as it is very difficult of access. People have climbed up there, however, but it is now forbidden on the ground of peril from the crumbling rock. See, they are beginning to settle down again."

Some of the feathered tribe seemed more slow to become tranquillized than others; but since there was no repetition of the disturbing roar, the whole colony was at rest once more before many minutes had elapsed.

Not long after the "Admiral" entered Gaspé Bay, which is about twenty miles in length, and at nine o'clock came to anchor in the Basin. Gaspé Basin, in one corner of which lies the town of the same name, is a land-locked sheet of water, four miles long and averaging half a mile across, a veritable salt lake shut in by mountains and verdant slopes, affording a perfect harbor to vessels seeking shelter from the high seas of the Gulf of St. Lawrence. The little town has one of the most charming situations to be found on the continent, and the entire party was in transports with the view, which in spite of the lateness of the hour was still apparent, so long is the twilight in this longitude during the early weeks of summer.

They were met at the wharf by a wiry, active-looking man with a brisk eye, who shook Colonel Russell heartily by the hand, and was introduced by him as "George Coffin, one of the best fellows in the world."

"And your servant, gentlemen," said the Canadian, who, be it said, had much of the Yankee in his build and manner.

"What are the chances for fish, George?" asked the Colonel.

"There's a terrible sight of salmon in the river," was the answer.

This sounded encouraging. Leaving George Coffin to collect the traps, and load them on a cart which he had brought for the purpose, the Colonel led the way up the wharf, past a line of villagers, for nearly every one of whom he had a word of greeting, stopping for a minute to exchange salutations with a red-faced old man with a pleasant, though somewhat leering smile, whom he addressed as Joe Eden.

"How has your health been, Joe?"

"Well, I'm not what I used to be, Colonel. But you ought to have come by the last steamer. We've had the governor-general here. He left only last night in his steam-yacht."

"Governor-general of what?" whispered Jack Hall to Mr. Holt.

"Of Canada."

"I am sorry I missed him," responded the Colonel.

" Ah, yes, " said the old man; " it is a pity!

"He was down to my shop," he added, indicating by a jerk of his thumb over his shoulder a low shanty-like building a few yards distant, "and he says to me, 'Joe, if you ever come to Ottawa, don't go to a hotel and wait for an invitation, but come right up to Rideau.' That's what I call hospitable."

This speech seemed to amuse the Colonel, who restrained his mirth by proceeding to introduce the whole party. "Mr. Eden is the collector of port of Gaspé, boys," he added.

"What's Rideau?" inquired Max as soon as they were out of hearing.

"The governor-general's residence at Ottawa," explained the Colonel, bursting into laughter. "Old Joe's a great character. Dickens would have found him a gold-mine."

At the top of the road leading down to the wharf was the main, and, in fact, the only street of the town, which followed the shore of the basin. Turning to the left, the Colonel soon branched off, and, after ascending a short lane bordered by green fields, knocked a moment after at the door of a comfortable-looking farm-house.

"It's you, Colonel, is it?" said the pleasant-voiced woman who came to the door. "Welcome to Gaspé."

"Glad to see you, Mrs. Dumaresque. I've

brought you an army of boys to eat you out of house and home. This is my friend Mr. Holt. Can you take care of us all?"

"There's always room for one more here, Colonel, if you'll put up with what we've got."

So saying, the calm but smiling hostess ushered them through the entry-way, which was ornamented with a huge pair of caribou horns, into a room where a table was spread for supper. A fine wood fire roared up the chimney at its further end. The blaze was welcome after the exposure to the cool night air. The boys gathered about the capacious hearth, and patted admiringly a large greyhound that rubbed against their legs in friendly fashion. Mrs. Dumaresque, who had vanished into the adjoining kitchen, reappeared presently with a dish of boiled salmon, followed by a maid with another of smoking cods' tongues and sounds.

"Supper is ready," she said.

Appetites were not wanting, and with good reason, for the fresh fish was supplemented by honest bread, new-laid eggs, and milk and cream such as only Jersey cattle can give. The Jersey merchants, in seeking an inhospitable shore, did not leave all their cows at home.

"Make the most of this, young gentlemen," said the Colonel, glancing around the table. "By this time to-morrow we shall be dependent on our own exertions for our daily food."

"Not quite so bad as that, surely," answered Mrs. Dumaresque with a quiet laugh. "You'll take a few Gaspé loaves and a basket of eggs, just to guard against accidents, you know. It wouldn't do to have you starve."

CHAPTER II.

THE FIRST NIGHT IN CAMP.

THE six boys were about the same age, between fifteen and sixteen. Jack Hall and Frank Haseltine were half way through their course at a large boarding-school in the country, concerning the advantages of which they were never weary of talking to the other four. Jack, who was a compactly built, sturdy-looking fellow, had ambition to win laurels as an oarsman, while "Hasy," as everybody called him, was already regarded as a base-ball player of great promise. In appearance Hasy was tall and rather lanky; but he had a bright, intelligent face and quaint, Western ways, that easily won him popularity. Dubsy Perkins was an old crony of Jack's, who in the days before Jack went to Utopia School had fought side by side with him in snow-ball fights in the streets of Boston, shared the glories

and disasters of the sports and pranks in which
they were mutually engaged, and had ever been,
and was still, one of his most ardent admirers.
Max, the elder of the two Fearings, though the
largest of the six, was rather fat and flabby looking. Neither he nor his brother had seen much
of other boys in the past, having been educated
until recently abroad. Joe, the younger, was a
sunny little lad, and both of them had excellent
manners; but their lack of knowledge on the
subject of sports had prevented them from becoming immediately intimate with the rest, who,
moreover, criticised them in private as stuck up,
and molly-coddled. Lastly, Tom Binney from
Philadelphia completed the party, — the happy
possessor of Bingo, a fox-terrier of minute pro-
portions. Tom had a fondness that amounted
almost to a passion for creatures, whether birds,
beasts, fish, reptiles, or insects; and he excited
much envy and admiration by announcing that
he had at home a bee-hive, eight rabbits, four
guinea-pigs, another pup, a parrot, a bat, three
snakes, a pony, an old hornet's nest, and an aquarium. As for Bingo, he was a prodigy: he would

stand on his legs for an indefinite period when ordered, jump through one's hands, pretend to be dead, and, apart from these interesting accomplishments, was a sworn foe of cats, and a nimble pursuer of squirrels.

The next morning was fine, and George Coffin was on hand immediately after breakfast with two buck-boards, on which to carry them about five miles, to where they were to take the canoes. On the vehicle which George drove himself were Jack, Haseltine, Tom Binney, and Max.

"Clck," said George, and the raw-boned white horse started off at a rattling rate, which soon caused the boys to hold on tight, while they wondered how such an ill-favored looking beast could be a trotter. The road followed the edge of the Basin; and along the way stretched a succession of small cottages, each with its few acres of land, which in most instances the farmer who owned it was tilling, seeking to make the most of the short season. Every thing looked green; and the sheep and the cows, though stunted and draggled by the hard winter, were evidently enjoying themselves.

"What are those?" asked Haseltine, pointing to a row of stakes connected by net-work, which ran out from the shore.

"A stand of nets," said George. "You'll see 'em right along every half mile or so. They're to catch the salmon with as they go up. The Government leases 'em to different parties."

"How do they catch them?" asked Tom, who was interested in anything that suggested a trap.

"The meshes are about the color of the water, and the fish in running up poke their noses into 'em, and get cotched by the gills when they try to back out."

"Doesn't it kill them?" asked Max with a shudder.

"No; it only holds 'em until some one comes along, and it doesn't hold 'em always, neither, for they break through sometimes. The critters are cute, too, about avoiding the nets. I've seen 'em smell their way through a two-foot passage, and I believe some of 'em would get through if the river was barred clear across."

"I'd like to take a live salmon home with me for my aquarium," said Tom.

"He'd die," said Jack stoutly, "for you said your aquarium is a salt one."

"Salt water wouldn't hurt a salmon," said George Coffin, "for they live in the salt water half the year. Salmon leave the river about September, and no one knows exactly where they go to. Some think they go into deep water, and some that they cruise about the coast. But come the last of May, and the ice out of the river, they're back running in by hundreds; and the curious thing is, they never make mistakes. There's three salmon rivers emptying into Gaspé Bay, and it's easy to tell the fish apart; but all the years I've been hauling nets, I never see a fish that belonged in one river in one of the other rivers."

"That's mighty funny," said Tom. "What do they ever leave the river for?"

"To find food. When a salmon runs into the river, he's fat as butter, and bright an' lively. But from then on he eats nothing, and gets more and more logy, until after spawning time he's peakish as a Gaspé sheep."

"Pshaw! Of course they eat something. How

could they live if they didn't eat anything?" exclaimed Jack incredulously. "You can't fool us."

"That's so!" said Haseltine.

"Gospel truth, young gentlemen. I've seen five hundred salmon cut open in this river if I've seen one, and I never found anything more'n a little yellow liquid inside any one of 'em. Take 'em now fresh run and you'll come across small fish and crabs, but after they've been in the river twenty-four hours there's nothing left in their stomachs."

"What do they rise at flies for?" asked Jack triumphantly.

"The only flies I ever see 'em eat is the artificial ones you anglers put on, and they're like no flies hereabouts. What makes the salmon rise to them's the strangest part of it. Some say it's anger, and some say it's curiosity. The trout, now, are different. There's no giving 'em enough to eat. Many's the greedy beggar I've caught, with a minnow most as big as himself in his gullet."

The boys pondered over these statements for

some moments; then Tom, winking at Jack, said, —

"I've got a puzzle I'd like to show you, Mr. Coffin, to see if you'd guess it."

Whereupon, Tom took a piece of paper and a pencil from his pocket, and proceeded to draw a large square, which, by a line across and a line down the middle, he divided into four smaller squares of the same size.

"There," he continued; "you'll have to pay close attention."

"Whoa!" said George Coffin to the trotter; and having pulled up the horse he turned round to inspect the diagram which Tom, who was on the back seat between Jack and Max, wished him to look at.

"A man had sixteen animals, horses, cows, sheep, and donkeys, — four of each kind, — and he had four plats of ground such as you see here. Into the first he put the four horses," said Tom, making as he spoke four marks with his pencil in the upper left-hand square to indicate the animals in question.

"The four horses," repeated George Coffin after him.

"Into the next he put the four cows, into the next the four sheep," continued Tom, making marks accordingly, "and into the fourth the four donkeys."

"Stop a minute," exclaimed George as Tom paused. "You have only put down three donkeys."

"Because you're the fourth," he answered gleefully; and the words were followed by a burst of laughter from the other boys, in which the victim joined as soon as he realized the situation.

"That beats anything I've heard this long time," said George, chuckling convulsively. "I rose for it greedy as a fresh run fish, and swallowed hook and all. I've got to look out for you boys, that's evident."

"We caught Max on it yesterday," said Jack. "He fell into the trap as easily as you did."

A few minutes later they stopped at a small house, from which a short, broad-shouldered man dressed in homespun came out to meet them. He invited the boys into his cabin, where his wife refreshed them with fresh milk and delicious bread and butter, and where they were presently joined by the rest of the party.

"Is it true, Colonel Russell," asked Jack between two mouthfuls, "that salmon eat nothing after they come into the river? George Coffin says so," he added, waggishly regarding the worthy Gaspé man.

"Perfectly true; and, moreover, you may believe everything that George tells you. He's too honest to deceive willfully even a baby.— You see these boys are accustomed to have jokes played on them at school," added the Colonel to his henchman, "and so are apt not to trust all they hear."

"And a fine joke they have just played on me," George replied, grinning from ear to ear.

Explanation caused renewed laughter, and then they set off for the river, which was but a few hundred yards from the house. George Coffin and William Annette brought down the lighter traps, which they arranged in two canoes in waiting, while the boys made the acquaintance of William Patterson, the Colonel's old guide, and his son Jimmy, a brawny, bushy-whiskered fellow.

George was to carry the main luggage into camp on a cart, and two of the boys were to go with him, as the canoes could not accommodate the whole party. Lots were drawn, and it fell to Haseltine and Dubsy to accompany George.

In the first canoe to start were Jimmy Patterson and Mr. Holt at bow and stern respectively, in order to paddle, and Jack and Tom side by side in the middle. The river at this point looked like a lagoon, being broad and sluggish, and intersected by strips of marshland on which horses and cows were feeding. The water was smooth as a mill-pond, and they passed a number more stands of nets, reaching out sometimes from one bank and sometimes from the other, so that it seemed as though the poor salmon would have to be very cunning to escape capture. Some of the nets had wings, as they were called, being extensions running at right angles down stream in order to cut off any fish that should see the danger and turn aside.

But after a time the river began to twist and to grow narrower and shallower. There were no more nets, and the farms were fewer in number and meaner in appearance. The land was covered with stumps of trees only partially burned away. Ahead the mountains loomed up in the distance. The air was softer, and the savor of the sea was gone. The current had become so strong that Mr. Holt and Jimmy, instead of continuing to paddle, turned the canoe in shore and took to poling.

Have you ever tried to pole a canoe? It may look easy, but it requires both muscle and knack to make a success of it on a salmon river. Mr. Holt evidently understood that he was in for warm work, as he stripped himself down to his flannel shirt before beginning. The poles were some eight feet long, and capped with iron points. They thrust them against the bottom on one side of the gunwale, and leaning on them shoved the canoe ahead by main force. At first it was a simple affair enough, but presently they came to places where the rocks below the surface caused the water to foam. These were rapids, and to get the canoe over them was no easy matter. Jack and Tom felt a little nervous at first, for fear of a ducking, but soon got used to the bumping and wobbling incident to climbing up stream. Meanwhile they asked all sorts of questions, which Jimmy Patterson was very amiable in answering.

"Are there bears in these woods?" asked Jack at the first opportunity. "I'd give anything to shoot a bear."

"Or catch a live cub," said Tom, whose fondness for live-stock was always uppermost.

"There's bear in plenty, and you might see one if you're lucky," answered Jimmy. "But winter's the time to come here hunting. The hills are full of caribou."

Just then they heard a whir, and a bird resembling a duck started up from the water ahead and flew past them, protruding its long neck and uttering a dismal squawking.

"If we'd only a gun handy, I'd make short work of you, my lady," said Jimmy, as he watched her scoot down the river for a few hundred yards and then alight. "Those ere noxious birds do more harm to the salmon in a season than fifty stand of nets," he added, turning the head of the canoe, and making a sudden but ineffectual dab with his pole.

"Oh, catch one, catch one, do!" cried Tom, who was the first to spy the brood of yellow fluffy ducklings struggling to reach the shore as fast as their feeble legs would carry them.

"Don't hurt them, Jimmy," urged Mr. Holt.

But the ducklings, despite their callowness, were nimble. Scattering in every direction they buried themselves in the underbrush at the margin before the canoe was able to overtake them.

"What were they?" asked the boys eagerly, when the last had disappeared.

"Shell-drakes. They live on the young salmon. If I were Colonel Russell, I'd offer a reward for every one that was shot, and clear the river," answered Jimmy.

"What made the mother bird desert them?" asked Tom.

"She thought in noticing her we should not see her brood until they had time to get out of the way, as was the case," said Mr. Holt.

As they proceeded, the rapids became more frequent and steeper, and sometimes the river ahead looked broken up into a foaming torrent. At these patches Jimmy and Mr. Holt hugged the shore pretty closely, and the clatter of their iron-shod poles against the rocks showed that progress was difficult. Every now and then the guide would call attention to some stretch of calmer water at the foot of a rough place as a pool where the fish lay. All these pools had their names. There was Miller's Landing and Gros Bouleau (which is French for Big Birch), and the Basket Pool and Dan's Hut, — the last so styled from a bark shanty on the bank in which the guardian of the river was in the habit of keeping look-out. In one or two of these Jimmy said that he could perceive salmon, and Jack and Tom were able to make out sundry dark streaks which he assured them were salmon. The boys were eager to begin fishing at once, but Mr. Holt declared that it was out of the question, for the rods were not unpacked, and every moment of time was needed in order to get the camp to rights before dark.

"You forget," said the master, "that there are trees to be cut down, and fires to be built, and tents to be pitched, and supper to be cooked."

"May I cut down the trees, Mr. Holt?" asked Jack.

"As many as you like, young man. But don't be too confident as to being able to supply us with fire-wood for the night by your unaided efforts. One has to learn even to cut down trees."

"I guess I've muscle enough," Jack answered with self-reliance, exhibiting his arm bent up, and patting the biceps.

They had started from Annette's at ten, and about four they came in sight of a low one-storied cabin, a few rods from the water, some thirty feet in length, surmounted by a flag-pole.

"There's the camp," cried Jimmy, to the great delight of the boys, who had been inquiring at intervals of five minutes during the past hour, as to when they would arrive. As they drew nearer, they perceived George Coffin and Dubsy and Haseltine awaiting them, the two last named waving their arms by way of welcome. Jack and Tom were delighted to step ashore, and to stretch their cramped legs in running up the slope to examine the little cabin, into which they were jubilantly ushered by their companions. There were two rooms, one supplied with bunks, and the other intended for a dining-room. The walls were covered with maps and fishing-scores and various newspaper cuttings of interest to sportsmen. Outside the prospect was very attractive. They were in the heart of the woods, and surrounded in the near distance by pine-clad mountains.

Over a circumference of several yards around the cabin the trees had been thinned out and the underbrush cleared away. There were rustic seats, and a table with a surface of smooth birch-bark surmounted by a rustic canopy, not far from which an accumulation of blackened stones marked the site of a fire-place. Beyond, as Dubsy, who had already made investigations, explained, was an ice-house full of frozen snow, in which George had bestowed the butter and eggs that had been brought in the cart.

The other canoe had arrived by this time, and the Colonel, accompanied by Max and Joe, came up the bank, followed by old William, who was grinning with pleasure at the sight of the six boys re-united. After a short consultation between Colonel Russell and Mr. Holt, it was decided that Mr. Holt and two of the boys should occupy the shanty, and that the rest of the party should be quartered in tents.

"I holloa to sleep in a tent," cried Jack.

"So do I," said Dubsy.

"The fairest way is to draw lots," suggested the Colonel; "though I warn the boys who sleep outside that it may be damp when it rains, to say nothing of the flies."

These did not seem to them very appalling considerations, though old William remarked casually, with a glance at the mosquito netting which protected the windows of the shanty, "The flies is awful wicked this time of year."

There were already a good many mosquitoes humming about their ears; but the boys were so intent on the plans for pitching camp, that they slapped their cheeks and brushed away the tormentors without much ado. Mr. Holt plucked six pieces of grass, which he clinched in his hand so as to let only the ends protrude. Whoever drew the shortest two were to remain in the cabin. Dubsy and Joe Fearing proved to be the unlucky ones, as it was so popularly considered. George

Coffin had unloaded the tents from the cart. There were three, — one for the Colonel, and the other two for the four boys. William Patterson and Jimmy were to sleep under a lean-to, where they would be protected from the rain and have the fire-place at their feet. As for George, he would spend the night in camp, but be off early in the morning.

The boys were much absorbed in trying to assist old William and George remove the tents from the bags in which they were packed, and select favorable sites for them.

In the mean time Mr. Holt was unstrapping the valises and untying the larger rubber bags containing their belongings, in order to get at the blankets which ought to be aired while the sun was still up. All was bustle and eagerness among the youthful helpers.

Of a sudden there came a distant hollow sound, repeated at regular intervals, which made them prick up their ears.

"What's that?" cried Jack.

"It's Colonel Russell and Jimmy chopping," said old William. "They be gone for logs."

"O Mr. Holt," cried Jack, "may I go and see them? You said I might cut down a tree."

"You may try certainly, Jack," was the answer. "But two of you are enough," Mr. Holt continued, as the whole six were on the point of taking advantage of this permission. "Jack and Hasy may go. I need the rest of you to help here. We should have a pretty state of things, if every time you saw or heard anything interesting you were all to drop work and go off in a body."

The two boys followed the direction from which the ringing of the axes proceeded, and in a few moments came in sight of the choppers, just as a magnificent maple was tottering.

"Look out — look out," cried the Colonel, who spied them, pointing as he shouted to the side to which they were to run.

The tree quivered irresolutely, as if hesitating which way to fall, and then came crashing down at a comfortable distance from where the two boys were standing. The Colonel and Jimmy leaning on their axes looked flushed and happy, as though they had enjoyed the exercise.

" Let me try," said Jack resolutely.

" You ? " said the Colonel with a laugh.

" Mr. Holt said I might."

" All right, Mr. Man," he replied, proffering the axe.

Jack received it with dignity, feeling a little nettled at the flippant tone manifested by his questioner. " Which one shall I cut down ? " he inquired coolly, as he swayed the weapon.

" You have the forest to choose from."

Jack put his left foot forward, and swinging the blade back over his shoulder, after a moment's hesitation in order to take aim, let drive with vim at a handsome mate to the prostrate maple. Somehow the effect produced was disappointing. The bark was wounded; but the blade, instead of cutting a deep gash, glanced off without doing further mischief.

Jack examined the edge critically. " Is it sharp ? " he inquired.

" I ground her last evening," said Jimmy, who also looked a little jocose.

Again Jack's foot went forward, and he smote with an air of determination, and with such effect that the blade at the end of the stroke was fast in the wood. Quickly extricating it, he braced himself firmly, and let drive once more. But so great was his energy that he must have misjudged his aim; for the axe merely grazed the trunk, and Jack went toppling over among the underbrush, to the great amusement of the others.

"Let's see you try," said the victim ruefully, as he picked himself up, addressing Haseltine.

But Haseltine shook his head. Like most American boys, he was not ashamed to admit that he could not do a thing. Both of them stood attentive while Jimmy, at the Colonel's suggestion, showed how a tree should be felled. In the first place, more muscle was needed than either of them at present possessed in order to cut down such a huge specimen as Jack had picked out except after much exertion. Then too there was knack about it, which became obvious as they watched the series of short, swiftly wielded strokes that made the chips fly. Little by little, Jimmy hewed out a great gap in the side of the maple. Then the Colonel put in a few alternate blows; and under the joint work of demolition, it

HE SMOTE WITH AN AIR OF DETERMINATION. — P. 49.

was not many minutes before the noble tree lay alongside its companion. The next thing was to lop off the boughs and strip away the branches. Out of the trunks they hewed famous logs for the fire-place and to serve as a frame-work to which to fasten the canvas stretchers provided for those who were to sleep in the tents. A few saplings supplied the best of tent-poles.

Jack and Haseltine assisted to carry the wood back to camp, and there was so much of it that they had to return for another load. Meantime a transformation scene was taking place. Sites had been chosen for the three tents a few feet from one another; and holes had been dug, in each of which an upright forked pole was fixed. There was a pole in front and a pole behind, and between the forks another cross pole, as it was called, was laid. Over this the canvas was spread, and fastened down at intervals of a foot or so to pegs driven in the earth. Old William appeared with his arms full of hemlock boughs, which he proceeded to strew over the ground inside of the tents, making a cool, green, and deliciously aromatic carpet. For the beds, first a rubber blanket was laid to keep out the damp, and then a sort of bedstead, manufactured from four logs placed at right angles, to which the stretchers referred to were tied; and on the stretchers one could lay hemlock and wraps to suit his fancy. By the time the tents were ready for occupancy, twilight was at hand, and every one was feeling hungry. Old William was to cook the supper this first evening, with Tom and Max as his assistants, or, more properly speaking, pupils. The others gathered about the Colonel, who was undoing some of his fishing-tackle. But interesting as was the exhibition, the boys found difficulty in keeping still, owing to the persistent torture of the mosquitoes and flies.

"Jiminy!" cried Jack, dancing from one leg to another. He had thrust his hands deep into his trousers' pockets, and had wound a handkerchief about his neck, but there were plenty of vulnerable spots left.

"What's the matter, Hall?" asked Colonel Russell, who was taking his best salmon rod out of its case with much the air that a young mother contemplates her baby.

"The mosquitoes are dreadful."

"I'm being eaten alive. It's agony," cried Dubsy, in confirmation of his friend.

"They've bitten through my stockings," said Haseltine.

"You should take off your low shoes, then," replied the Colonel, in answer to the last exclamation. "You can't expect the flies not to bite your feet if you don't take proper precautions. They are pretty wicked though to-night, that's a fact," he continued, making a pass with his hand to interrupt a mosquito that was feasting on his forehead. "You boys wait a minute, and I'll fix you all right.—Here, Jimmy," he cried, "start up a smudge."

"What's a smudge?" asked Jack, in whom the appetite for information was not dulled by present discomfort.

"A fire of damp wood and leaves or bark, that'll make a smoke. It drives away the flies," said the Colonel, who was unstrapping his fishing-box.

"I feel as if red-hot little pins were being stuck into me all over," cried Jack, waving his arms savagely to drive away the pests. "Get away, oh, get away!"

"Them's sand-flies," said Jimmy. "'Bite 'em no see 'em,' that's what the Injuns call 'em, because they're so small."

The boys looked at their hands. "What! those little black specks?"

"Yes, those are sand-flies," said the Colonel, who had produced a round tin can, "and they're terrible torments, too, — more so than even the black fly or mosquito. They are worst at sunset or sunrise. But put on some of this, and the whole tribe will fight shy of you," he continued, removing the cover of the can, and revealing some sticky looking stuff about the color of molasses, and the consistency of liquid glue, a dab of which he proceeded to rub over his cheeks, along his nose, around his neck, and behind his ears, with considerable gusto.

"It looks very nasty," said Mr. Holt, who had just then joined the group.

"It smells like tar," said Jack, taking a sniff at the can.

"There's tar in it, and oil and pennyroyal, and it *is* rather nasty until you get used to it; but there's nothing like it for keeping off the flies," said the Colonel, exhibiting his face which was now several degrees darker than usual, giving him much the appearance of an oily Indian. "Next?"

"No, thank you. I'll put up with the flies a little longer," exclaimed Mr. Holt.

"I'll give you just five minutes after the sand-flies fairly get to work, and at the end of it you'll be begging for some, on your bended knees, my dear fellow."

"You forget that I've been in the woods before."

"But not in these woods. Just mark my words,—that's all I ask of you."

"How do you put it on?" asked Jack, after another cautious sniff.

"Dip your fingers in, and take some. What are you waiting for, a silver spoon?"

Jack obeyed the instruction, and began to

anoint himself, to the intense interest of the others, who, one by one, followed his example.

"There," said the Colonel, surveying the copper-colored quartette complacently, "with the fishing-gloves which Mr. Holt has brought you to protect your hands, I think you'll do."

By this time the smudge was smoking finely, and the boys were just being initiated in regard to rods and reels, when the cry of "supper!" reminded them that they had forgotten they were hungry. As the twilight was so pleasant, it had been decided to have it served on the table out of doors, whither Max and Tom, in the proud capacity of embryo waiters, were bearing the variety of tempting edibles which they had helped to cook. Despite Mr. Holt's remark that to eat salmon which none of them had caught was unsportsmanlike, every one, he included, consumed with a rousing appetite the piece of fine fish Mrs. Dumaresque had provided them with in order that they need not starve. There were fried potatoes, too, and fried eggs, and the same Gaspé bread and butter which had tasted so well the night before, and hot tea

with real cream, so that they might not at one
fell swoop be separated from the luxuries of
civilization; and, last but not least, large, doughy
flap-jacks, which Jimmy not inappropriately spoke
of as "choke-dogs." How good everything
tasted, and how heartily they ate! Not only
the boys, but Mr. Holt and the Colonel, too,
showed themselves such famous trenchermen,
that Max and Tom were glad to be released
from the fear that, if they were kept waiting
much longer, there would be nothing left.

Before the meal was over, it was growing
dusk, and jimmy lighted two lanterns, which cast
quaint shadows around the banquet board, but
encouraged the mosquitoes to even greater energy
in the way of getting mixed up with the food,
and drowned in the tea. Thanks to the Colonel's
mixture, every one but Mr. Holt was enabled
to keep the humming torments at a respectful
distance. He, poor man, having affected for a
long time to be indifferent to their attacks, at
last, in a sudden burst of suppressed irritation,
sprang up, exclaiming, "Where's the nasty stuff?
I can't endure this torture any longer."

This complete triumph of the Colonel, as well
as of the mosquitoes, set every one laughing.
The boys all followed their master into the
shanty to behold the smearing process. He took
his revenge upon them, however, as soon as he
was anointed, by suggesting overcoats. The
air had become decidedly chilly; and even the
Colonel, after lighting his pipe, directed his steps
toward the crackling fire of logs which the guides
had started. Jack and Dubsy were deputed to
learn the mysteries of dishwashing, but the rest
of the party composed themselves around the
blaze. The boys, sitting in a row with their
knees drawn up to their chins, put one in mind
of a detachment of wolves. They were, one and
all, entranced with their surroundings. On every
side the tall trees, shrouded in shadow, supplied
a mysterious gloom, the weird effect of which
was heightened by the melody of the rushing
river. High above their heads the sky was
bright with stars. Old William and George and
Jimmy had each some interesting anecdote to
tell of former experiences, either in the way of
salmon fishing or canoeing or hunting expedi-

tions in the winter-time after caribou; in return for which the Colonel recalled wonderful adventures with wild boars and tigers that aroused every one's enthusiasm. It required, indeed, old William's query, "At what hour will you start in the morning, sir?" to remind them of time and the present.

"Yes, we must see about that," said the Colonel. "What are we to do to-morrow, Holt? You are the chief cook and grand master here. We have two canoes and six boys. How are we to manage?"

"We shall have to take turns about fishing, of course," said Mr. Holt. "Some of us must look after the camp. I suggest that you and old William and one of the boys go up or down river as you see fit, and that Jimmy take two more with him, and go in the opposite direction. The boys that go with Jimmy are to be taught how to pole as well as how to fish. I and the other three will look after things here."

"That sounds well," said the Colonel; and after some further talk it was. arranged that little

Joe Fearing was to go with him, and Jack and Haseltine with Jimmy.

It was ten o'clock by this time, which was very late for camp, Mr. Holt declared, and the boys were consigned to bed, to which, in spite of their fatigue, they were loath to go. Tom and Max were to sleep in one tent, and Jack and Haseltine in another. By Mr. Holt's advice, they had all been fitted out before starting with so-called Norfolk jackets, which as most of you know are plaited blouses belted round the waist. Under these were waistcoats and colored flannel shirts worn over thin under-flannels. Most of them had knickerbockers instead of ordinary trousers, and strong laced boots. For the night, although it seemed a little shivery proceeding, they took off everything and donned pjamahs. Each of them was supplied with a famous pair of blankets in which to roll himself, and from a framework of saplings a mosquito-netting hung down so as to cover each stretcher.

"Now, Jack," said the Colonel, who, in company with the master, was superintending the housing of the boys in turn, "you'd better make sure there are no flies under your canopy before we put out the light. The beggars are sly, and know enough to keep quiet and hide themselves in the corners of the netting. I've always found the best way to prove that there are none left is to place the lantern beside your bare big toe, and wait."

This suggestion appealed immensely to Jack and Haseltine, who had just crept under the netting as circumspectly as possible, after having removed the fly-oil from their faces and hands by dint of somewhat laborious scrubbing, and who were therefore in an unprotected condition. They proceeded accordingly to follow the directions given, first, however, making a preliminary search with lanterns all over their prison-cells, during which they succeeded in detecting and slaying several low-lying, able-bodied mosquitoes. But now each lay still, with one of his big toes exposed to attack close beside the light of the candle. The Colonel and Mr. Holt with smiling faces stood looking on in silence in the open space between the two stretchers. For some moments there was perfect stillness in the tent; but just as Jack was beginning to think that the enemy was entirely shut out, a large fellow stealthily descended from the top of the netting, and after a gyration or two above the tempting lure alighted. Quick as a cat, Jack leaned forward, and by a clever clap of the hands ended the existence of the miniature vampire, which, startled from its feast, was seeking to escape by flight. In the vehemence of his movements he managed, however, to upset and extinguish his lantern, which suggested to the seniors the advisability of bringing the still hunt to an end. They went out, carrying with them the other lantern.

"Good-night, boys."

"Good-night, Mr. Holt. Good-night, Colonel Russell."

During several minutes Jack and Haseltine chatted merrily, discussing the events of the day; but by degrees the conversation flagged, and Jack on his part became fascinated by the stillness of the woods. Every sound was strangely distinct. The river was rushing on with the same hoarse murmur, and every now and then there came cries from afar, which he associated with beasts and birds. The noise of a charred log falling in the smoldering fire sounded like a thud. Instead of being sleepy, he felt wide awake. Little by little the camp noises died away. All the party had gone to bed, and near at hand only the embers kept up a low sputtering. He wondered if the river never got tired of running on and on without a pause. How pleasant the smell of the hemlock boughs was! He raised himself on his elbow, and listened.

He could hear his companion's regular breathing. "Hasy," he whispered; but Haseltine was in the Land of Nod. So he lay down, and composed himself in his blanket. He was warm and comfortable; why did he not sleep? Perhaps it was the tea. He began to wonder what a bear would do if it should run across the camp. Hark! what was that? He raised himself again to listen. There was a loud crackling of the twigs close at hand, and he could hear the stamping of feet. How his heart was beating! The creature, whatever it was, was perambulating around the tent. Now it was on Haseltine's side. Could it be a bear, or a caribou, or a wildcat? It must be large, for it made a terrific tramping. If he only had a gun! What ought he to do? To call for help seemed cowardly. The noise had stopped now, and everything was still. Where could the beast be? All of a sudden a cold tremor seized him, and he shook like an aspen. Right in the doorway of the tent, where the flap was folded in a little so as to leave an opening, were two fierce, blazing eyes fixed upon him. That was all he could see.

Jack dared not stir. Thank heavens! he was not unarmed. Instinctively he reached out for his sheath-knife, which from an impulse of caution he had laid beneath his stretcher before getting into bed. He remembered to have read that wild beasts will quail under the steady glance of man, and he resolved that no shrinking on his part should be an incen- tive to the animal to leap upon him. He stared into the fiery eyes with all his ability. They were a greenish yellow. They must belong to a wildcat. "Cats" old William had called them, in a blood-curdling tone, in speaking after supper of their treacherous qualities. Of a sudden he heard his companion stir.

"Hasy," he murmured again hoarsely.

"What is it?"

"Look — see there."

The consciousness that an ally was close at hand gave Jack courage, and, as he spoke, he started to get out of bed, knife in hand; but he had forgotten the mosquito - netting. His progress was rudely barred, and before he could extricate himself the eyes had vanished.

"What is it?" Haseltine was asking. He had seen nothing.

But Jack, having crawled out of his bed, proceeded valiantly to throw aside the tent-flap and step outside. He clasped his knife firmly, with the intention, and almost with the hope, of engaging in a hand-to-hand encounter with the disturber of his rest. He looked stealthily about him. It was lighter than when he had gone to bed, for the moon though on the wane was up, and the open expanse which lay between him and the river was clearly illuminated. He could see nothing, nor could he hear a sound except the beating of his own heart.

"What are you up to, Jack?" he heard Haseltine inquire.

Just then there was a stirring to the left,— a repetition of the same tramping noise. He looked eagerly in the direction from which it proceeded. The tramping ceased, and he perceived sitting on its hind legs erect and motionless in the moonlight a large hare. For a moment the twain exchanged contemplative glances, then the quadruped by a series of bounds such as had served to excite its adversary's keen apprehension a little before disappeared in the underbrush.

"Swanny!" said Jack under his breath.

"What's the matter?" asked Haseltine, who, having also had a tussle with the mosquito-netting, had only just got upon his feet.

"I thought I heard a bear mousing round the tent," answered Jack reflectively, "but I guess it must have been my imagination."

"Did you see anything?" asked Haseltine.

"I saw what looked like a pair of eyes, but a fellow is always liable to be mistaken."

"Perhaps it was a nightmare."

"Yes, I guess on the whole it must have been," Jack answered eagerly. "Those choke-dogs must have disagreed with me. Good-night."

CHAPTER III.

"HIM BRIGHT SALMON."

SALMON fishing, unlike some other kinds of fishing, does not require particularly early rising; that is to say, it is not necessary to get up before the sun in order to be successful. One can defer, indeed, with advantage reaching the fishing-ground until the lamp of day has climbed above the tree-tops sufficiently to light up the dark pool; for the salmon are chary about rising, in the piscatorial sense of the word, until certain that night is gone. If one begins to cast by eight o'clock on a bright morning, it is time enough for an angler content to take life easily.

Colonel Russell was of this sort. There was no one more ready to be up with the lark (since authorities unite in fixing on that bird as the earliest of all risers), if by so doing he could gain any advantage in the way of sport; but, as he explained to the party at breakfast, he had never been able to see the advantage of a very early start merely from bravado. He was in excellent spirits, as was indeed every one. The day was clear, and gave promise of not being too warm. The boys had slept soundly, and were loud in their praises of camp life. Even Jack had passed a comfortable night, all things considered; but he was feeling a little anxious this morning as to what Haseltine might let out regarding the bear. They had been waked at six, and a sponge bath at the river brink had proved very refreshing, although the sand-flies took advantage of so favorable an opportunity to do some savage biting, and the water was still icy in consequence of the but lately melted snows. Several of the boys were eager to plunge into the river in order to prove their ability to defy the current after the manner of Horatius; but Mr. Holt issued a general order to the effect that no one should venture beyond his knees, which put a stop to such aspirations for the time being. Breakfast was prepared by Mr. Holt and Dubsy, while Max was taken under Jimmy's wing to receive a lesson in wood-chopping. No one was to be idle. Those who fished to-day would work on the morrow. Meanwhile, the fortunate ones were absorbed in arranging the tackle, concerning which Jack, Haseltine, and Joe were equally and profoundly ignorant. Mr. Holt had provided them each with a rod, a reel, a silk line one hundred and fifty yards in length, and a book of flies. With eager eyes they watched the Colonel put together his split bamboo, smearing the ferrule of each joint with soap, in order that it might come apart easily when he should wish to take it to pieces.

"That's a stunning pole," said Jack.

"A what?" asked the Colonel.

"A stunning fishing-pole."

"Call it a rod, young man — call it a rod. When you go perching or pickereling with clams or mummy-chunks for bait, you may call the stalwart instrument by means of which you yank the fish out of the water a fishing-pole if you like. But this," he said, — exhibiting with pride his seventeen-foot bamboo, which, as he swayed it, looked all nerves and sensibility — "is a rod, if you please."

Every one laughed; but Jack's mortification was only momentary, so much interested was he in the preparations. He, as did the others, took the rod into his hands to see how beautifully it was balanced. It was of a straw color, well polished and in four joints, including the tip, which appeared very delicate and flexible.

"I should think a big fish would break that off snap," said Hasy.

"Many's the thirty-pound salmon I've landed with it," said the Colonel. "I never broke but one tip, and that was because the fish — only a small one, too, — ran under the canoe. You see the strain is regulated by the reel. Very little pressure will start it," he said, producing a large rubber reel which he proceeded to fasten on just above the butt. Then he gave a pull at the line, which ran off with a whir that thrilled the boys.

"There's no music more pleasant to a sportsman than that," he continued, as he passed the oiled silk line along the rod through the rings provided for it, and brought it down again to within a yard from his hands, after which he rested the rod against one of the tent-poles, and asked Joe to fetch him a cup of water. While this was being brought, the Colonel took out a tin box from one of the partitions of his fishing-case, which was subdivided with a view to holding his tackle conveniently. This proved to contain a number of flat square paper packages. In the upper one of these was a collection of coils of white cat-gut.

" Casting-lines," he said, forestalling a question. He picked out three of these, and after undoing the kinks dropped them into the cup of water which had just arrived. "They have to be soaked before they're used, or they're liable to snap," he continued.

In the other package there was an assortment of artificial flies which the Colonel opened for in-spection. These were of different sizes, according to the size of the hook, but the few which the Colonel selected to put in his fly-book were not larger than big trout flies. They were made up of various colors, some gaudy and others modest, not to say dull; and they had curious names such as " Jock Scott," " Silver Doctor," " Fairy,"

"Butcher," and "Cock Robin," to the enumeration of which the boys listened with wide-open mouths.

"Which shall you fish with to-day?" asked little Joe.

"A 'Jock Scott' to begin with. That's about the best fly in the long run. If they won't take that, they're very apt to refuse everything."

The "Jock Scott" was one of the prettiest and most brilliant, having a black and orange body, and a wing made up of feathers from the jungle-cock, the blue macaw, the golden pheasant, and a number of other birds.

The Colonel after waiting a few moments took one of the casting-lines out of the water. It was soft and flexible now. Putting its loop through the eye of the Jock Scott, he fastened them together. Then he picked up what looked like a brass thermometer with a great hook at the end of it, and interlocking it with the barb of the fly, said to Jack, —

"Take the other end of the casting-line in your hand, and after it is taut pull on it gently until I tell you to stop."

Jack obeyed orders.

"A little harder."

The gut was stretched tightly now, and the others, who were looking at the scales in the Colonel's hand, could see the indicator move.

"A little harder."

"It's up to seven," said Hasy impressively.

"A little harder."

Again the indicator moved a trifle, and then suddenly re-acted with a click. Jack found himself with a piece of the casting-line in his grasp, staring in bewildered surprise. It had snapped in two.

"Bah!" said the Colonel. "It ought to stand eight pounds, though it would never have such a strain. It's a very difficult matter to get first-rate gut." The next proved to be a better piece; and the Colonel as he fastened it to the silk line explained, in answer to an inquiry on the part of Joe, that the casting-line was used because it was so nearly the color of the water that it escaped the notice of the fish. Just then Jimmy appeared with some fine twine which he was waxing vigorously. This proved to be for Jack's rod, which was a spliced one ; that is to say, the joints, instead of fitting into one another in socket fashion like those of the Colonel’s, had to be laid over one another and tied together. It was of green-heart, which many consider even more springy and satisfactory than the bamboo, while very much more inexpensive. Splicing is quite a lengthy process, for the twine has to be wound exactly and tightly ; and while Jimmy was showing Jack how to do it, the Colonel and Mr. Holt put together the rods for Hasy and Joe, which were of lancewood. All the rods had been selected by Mr. Holt under Colonel Russell’s supervision, and the Colonel, upon examining each with a critical eye after they were ready for use, pronounced himself unable to say which seemed the best, they were all so well proportioned and supple. He even declared that there was very little to choose between any one of them and his own precious bamboo, though to be sure they were all a foot shorter, in order to suit the stature of the boys.

“ There’s only one disadvantage about a spliced rod,” he added, as he manipulated Jack’s, “the trouble there is in taking it apart, or rather in putting it together, which is sometimes inconvenient. But for the balance and limber action, there is nothing to surpass it. That's a beautiful rod, young man, — not pole, please take notice."

By the time all was ready for departure, it was eight o'clock. Old William and Jimmy had each cut a stout stick, and firmly set into it one of the gaffs produced by the Colonel from his tent, — vicious looking steel hooks, whose sharp points were protected by corks for the time being. Mr. Holt and the three boys who were to stay behind went down to the water's edge to see the anglers off.

"Good-by. Good luck."

A moment later the swiftly gliding canoe passed round the bend in the river, leaving the Colonel and Joe on the point of coming to anchor at the Camp pool, which they were to fish before going up.

"Isn't it fun?" said Jack, as they flew along on the swift current.

"Glorious!" murmured Haseltine.

After about ten minutes Jimmy stopped paddling abreast of a high bank on one side of the stream just at the foot of a steep rapid, and lifting the stone tied to a rope which he had beside him for an anchor dropped it softly into the water.

"Is it a pool?" asked Jack.

"Yes, the High Bank, and a likely place to get salmon," the guide replied as he paid out the necessary slack.

The boys grasped their rods eagerly; but, as Jimmy explained to them, it was out of the question for both of them to fish at the same time. They must cast turn and turn about, each for a little while and then the other. He would show them how, for casting was no easy matter to learn. So Jack relinquished his green-heart, and watched Jimmy unwind a few yards of line by holding the tip close to the water after the current had taken the fly, and jerking it gently until the reel started. When some six or eight yards had been thus freed and carried down river, he suddenly flung the rod with both hands, so that the point went straight up into the air a little over one shoulder, and the line flew far behind; then after a scarcely perceptible pause brought the rod back again by a quick yet deliberate sweep and turn of the wrist, in such a way that the fly came shooting forward and alighted on the surface first as lightly as a feather.

"You should cast across the current, not dead ahead. In that way your **fly** 'll be carried down so as to look natural."

After the line had swung round so that it was running straight down stream, Jimmy let out another few inches from the reel, and cast again. This he repeated at intervals of about a minute.

"Feel a bite?" asked Hasy.

"Salmon rise, they don't bite," observed Jack sententiously.

"How do you know?"

"Because I heard Colonel Russell say so."

"You needn't talk, anyway, with your 'fishing-pole.'"

"Ancient history," retorted Jack. He was pleased to have an opportunity to get even with Hasy; for, devoted friends as they were at boarding-school, there was naturally a generous rivalry between them. But it was scarcely prudent of him, all the same, in view of the episode of the night before. "Let sleeping dogs lie," — to say nothing of bears, — is an excellent motto.

"You wait, that's all," said Hasy enigmatically after a pause, too intent evidently in watching Jimmy cast to indulge in further repartee, yet wishing to give warning that he reserved the right of renewing the colloquy at some future time. Meanwhile, although the line flew out famously, and the fly lighted noiselessly as one could desire, there was no sign of a fish.

"Let me try now," said Jack. "I guess I can cast all right."

"I'll reel in some first. You'd better begin with a short line," said Jimmy.

Jack stood up with his legs a little apart as he had seen Jimmy do, and grasped the rod with both hands, one above the reel and one below it.

"Be careful now not to tumble over and upset the canoe," said Jimmy by way of caution.

The experience with the axe had given Jack somewhat less confidence in his ability to accomplish wonders off-hand in untrodden fields, but pride forbade him to suggest the possibility of failure.

"How shall I know when a salmon bites — I mean rises?" he added hastily.

"Smarty!" observed Haseltine with a short laugh.

"You'll know fast enough. Be careful not to jerk the fly out of his mouth, though, when you feel him. He'll hook himself nine times in ten, but it's just as well to turn your wrist a bit at first. Easy, easy, or you'll scare every fish in the pool," Jimmy added, as line, casting-line, and fly fell in a bunch on the surface with a splash. Jack had lashed with the rod as though it were a base-ball bat, so anxious was he to make a long cast. The second time he was much more deliberate, and though the line and fly alighted simultaneously it was without noise. He followed Jimmy's directions to let the current take the fly as far as it would, and to undulate the rod slightly in order to produce the effect of an insect moving. He then made several casts, which were so far successful that the fly reached the water in the end, which without elating him gave him a little self-reliance. After every one of these casts he let out a few inches more line, until there was now almost as much out as Jimmy had used. There was still no sign of a fish.

"Cast across a little farther. They may be lying on that side of the pool," said Jimmy.

Jack loosened another bit of line, and clinching his teeth cast with some vim, intending to cover new ground; but as he started to propel the fly forward after the upward sweep he was suddenly all but pulled off his feet, and the tip of his rod was bent violently backwards.

"You've got a big fellow this time," said Jimmy with a laugh.

Jack certainly had. His fly was caught in one of the branches of a tree that projected out from the shore overhead. "That's a bite, not a rise, I guess," said Haseltine with a chuckle.

Jack was so nettled by the misadventure that he began to pull and jerk somewhat roughly on the line; but Jimmy took it from his hand, and after a few moments managed to shake it free.

"All right now," said Jimmy, throwing the fly overboard.

But our hero was doomed to further discomfiture.

Scarcely had he got to work again, than, in an attempt to be deliberate, his Jock Scott came in contact with the water behind, which caused — although he tried his best to overcome the extra drag on the tip — the line to fall in a tangle about his ears, and the hook to catch in the side of the canoe. This was too much for his patience. He ground his teeth, and perceiving a provoking smile on Haseltine's face exclaimed, —

"If you think it's so easy, try yourself."

It was rather a new experience to Jack to be foiled in a matter of this sort. He was naturally handy and clever at sports, and he and Haseltine were beginning decidedly to be cocks at the great school to which they belonged, on account of their prowess. Perhaps this had begotten an idea in their minds that they could do anything with very little trouble. Certainly, the dual experience of wood-chopping and casting must have shaken that theory somewhat in Jack's mind at least. He now beheld, moreover, Haseltine manipulating the rod in a much more facile manner than he had done, casting quite with an experienced air, as became one who had caught many a brook trout by dint of a tree branch, a thread, and a pin tipped with worm. Jack's piscatorial exploits, on the other hand, had been confined to salt water, requiring a much bolder style of angling and coarser materials. As Jimmy endeavored to impress, force is a quality that needs to be used very charily in fly-fishing, and Haseltine seemed to appreciate that from the start. He used a short line, and after a few moments of difficulty succeeded in making the fly trip gracefully forward just in time to forestall the line and drop deftly on the water. He handled his rod knowingly, too, and did not seem to be discountenanced by the reel, which is not a very easy protuberance to get accustomed to. He brought the tip round so as to make the fly move entirely to the satisfaction of Jimmy, who was now keenly on the lookout for a rise.

All of a sudden, just as Haseltine started to make a cast, there came a whir from the reel, and the tip bent toward the water.

"What did I tell you?" cried Jimmy.

" Is it a salmon?" asked Hasy, who, trembling with excitement, threw up the point of his rod

as he had been directed to do, and began to reel
in the line.

Somehow, the fish was exceedingly tranquil
after the first haul. The line had become taut,
owing to the reeling; but whatever was at the
other end of it chose to make no further demonstration. There was something there, however,
which seemed to Hasy very unyielding.

"Is it a salmon?" he inquired again feverishly,
in answer to which Jimmy, whose expression had
gradually changed to a sickly grin, responded
laconically, "You're fast to the bottom of the
river."

As may be imagined, this was delightful news
to Jack, who had been perhaps rather nettled at
his rival's skill, and who was now able to laugh
until his side ached.

"You want the earth, Hasy. You've got it
this time, ha, ha!"

Examination proved that the hook had caught
in a snag, an old root sticking up from the
bottom.

"You let your fly sink too deep; that was
the trouble," observed Jimmy. "I thought you

had a whale by the way it took hold at first. I reckon we'll quit this, and try Dan's hut for a spell. Funny, too, there ain't no fish here this time of year. We'd ought to have had one landed by this time."

The boys felt a little gloomy, for they also had expected better things. Jimmy hauled up the stone, and as they glided across the pool peered over the edge of the canoe.

"There isn't one of the beggars there," he said.

It was only a short run to Dan's hut. As they came abreast of the shanty, they perceived lying on the bank in front of it a yellow-skinned looking fellow, smoking a pipe, who had much the aspect of an Indian. At sight of him, Jimmy gave a significant grunt.

"Who's that?" asked Jack.

"Pete Labouisse."

"Is he an Indian?"

"His mother was a squaw. He's a half-breed."

Jack had seen Indians before, having visited their encampments in summer to buy straw baskets and bows and arrows; but that was a very different affair from beholding the red man in his native forest. A vision of tomahawks, scalps, and war paint, arose vividly before his imagination, the completeness of which was somewhat marred by the consciousness that Pete was attired very much like other people at Gaspé, except more shabbily.

"What's he doing here?" inquired Haseltine.

"No good, you may be sure of that," answered Jimmy wisely.

"Say," he continued, shouting through his hands to the object of his criticism, "seen a one jump?"

"Ya, ya!" responded the Indian gutturally, between the puffs. "Bright salmon."

"Copper-colored fox!" muttered Jimmy. "I'd wager something he's had a slice of one for breakfast. Some day, old boy, we'll catch you at your tricks, and then look out."

"I don't see his rod," said Hasy innocently.

"What would he be doing with a rod? No sirree, a pine knot and a spear are good enough for him; and he'd catch more'n a single night than the Colonel with his whole book of flies in a week. That's what they call flambeauing, and it's death on the fish."

"What is it he does?" asked Jack, curious as to the precise nature of the wickedness in question.

"Does?" echoed Jimmy, who was letting down the stone. "Why, he waits for a dark night, and goes sneaking over the pools with a torch. The salmon come swimming up to see what the light means, and it's easy enough then to stick a spear through 'em. It weren't many years ago that the rivers all over Canada were nearly emptied of fish because of the flambeauing; and it costs a good spell in jail if one gets caught at it now. But what's to prevent a chap like Pete from saying he's going up river trapping, and then biding his time?"

This explanation was cut short by a cry from Jack, who pointed eagerly ahead of the canoe. A silver gleam embodying a fine fish was for a moment perceptible, followed by a splash which sent the ripples flying.

"So you're there, are you?" exclaimed Jimmy. "Pete hasn't got 'em all, anyhow."

At the same moment the half-breed gave vent

to another guttural utterance, as much as to say, "I told you so." The boys were in a fever of excitement; and Jack, who it had been agreed on the way down from the High Bank pool should be the first to cast, was trembling so that he could hardly hold the rod.

"Wasn't he a beauty!" he ejaculated. "What did he weigh, Jimmy?"

"Close on thirty pounds."

"What made him jump out of the water?"

"Playing. They often do."

"Do you believe he'll take my fly?"

"There's no telling. When they act like that, they'll sometimes take a fly, and sometimes not. Let your line out gradual now. Don't be in a hurry to reach him," Jimmy added.

For some minutes there was rapt silence. Jack cast and cast again with all the care and skill he could muster, but not a sign of a fish appeared. He combed the pool, as anglers say, from top to bottom, until all the anchor rope was exhausted. Jimmy got the canoe back to the starting-point as quietly as possible, and suggested putting on a Silver Doctor in place of the

Jock Scott. By this time the boys were looking rather sombre. They had felt confident of hooking the salmon that had jumped. What could the matter be? The fly must have passed over his nose a dozen times. However, it would never do to despair so early, and Jack began to cast again with a determined manner; but the Silver Doctor appeared to be as little appreciated as the Jock Scott. Not a fish rose, and even Jimmy wagged his head, and said, " It beats the Dutch."

Just as he spoke, Jack cast again wearily. The fly now reached to the farthest extremity of the pool, and there seemed little use in watching it. An instant later there was an exclamation from Pete on the bank, who pointed eagerly at the water; and simultaneously Jimmy cried, " You've got him. Don't jerk."

Jack, following the Indian's gesture, had seen a large swirl close to where his fly might well be; and, as he heard Jimmy's voice, he felt the line tighten. Obeying the caution given, he simply held his rod firm. It was apparent to him that the fish was going down. The next moment his reel was whirring violently, and his line running out at a tremendous rate.

"Keep the point of your rod up, keep the point of your rod up, or you'll lose him," he heard Jimmy cry excitedly; and he tried to do so, though the fish was making such a stir that it was not very easy. At last he got it up at a tolerable angle, with the result of checking the violent rush, owing to the greater purchase thus acquired. The fish had come to a halt, though he was pulling so steadily that the tip was bent well down. Jack could feel a sort of thrumming or vibration along the line, which thrilled him with satisfaction.

"Is it a salmon?" he asked.

"It's a salmon, and a big one," answered Jimmy.

"Hooray," cried Haseltine.

Delighted as he was, Jack felt almost helpless. He was in utter ignorance as to what he should do. Ought he to reel or to pull harder? How much strain would the rod stand?

"Am I doing all right?" he asked feverishly.

"Yes. Give him the butt, though." Then,

seeing that Jack looked puzzled, he added, "I mean keep the butt of your rod out, and the tip up. The moment he weakens, reel on him." Jimmy had pulled up the stone, and was holding the canoe by means of his pole, evidently prepared for whatever might happen.

"Am I to go ashore?" Jack asked.

"Not yet," said Jimmy grimly. "Look out."

Just then, as a consequence of receiving the butt, the fish started on another rush more violent than the first, which made the reel sing shrilly, and broke down Jack's guard completely. Then to the left, but not twenty yards away, something leaps a foot out of water. What is that? his fish? It cannot be. Yet is not Jimmy crying, "Lower your rod! lower your rod"?

"Him bright salmon, him bright salmon," shouts Pete, wakened to enthusiasm.

But Jack scarcely heeds the tidings. He has lowered his rod, and, after doing so, realizes that the line, instead of being taut, is slack and loose; it has ceased to run out. The rod is wobbling. Is the salmon lost? is he off? As the terrible thought suggests itself, he feels a hollow sinking of the stomach unlike any thing he has ever felt before. Then he hears close at hand, —

"Reel — reel — reel."

He reels with all his might. Surely the fish is gone. Where can he be? There is no strain on the line. But still he reels, while Jimmy hastily shoves the canoe up river and toward the shore, in order, as Jack later learns, to prevent the salmon from running under it: for the sly monster has dashed up stream, as is immediately manifest by his leaping out of water again, and this time nearly abreast of the canoe.

"Him bright salmon — him bright salmon."

Still again he leaps; and this time Jack gets a good glimpse of him, and realizes what has happened. It is his fish.

"Reel — reel — reel," reiterates Jimmy.

Is he not reeling as hard as he can? especially now that he understands that the salmon is still on. What a splendid fellow he is! How silvery and beautifully shaped! Oh, he must save him! Where is he now? He can feel him

"LOWER YOUR ROD! LOWER YOUR ROD!"—P. 93.

distinctly, for the line is getting taut. Ah, yes, he is pulling steadily, and taking another breathing spell! Hurrah! he is not lost.

Now that Jack feels again the steady strain, and is conscious of the thrumming, he too has a chance to take breath, of which he is quite as much in need as the salmon. The perspiration is streaming down his cheeks, and he tastes tar oil in his mouth. His hands, too, are slippery from the same causes, and he reflects that he ought to have worn his fishing gloves as advised by the Colonel. It is impossible to put them on now without passing his rod to Jimmy or Haseltine, which he would not do for a five-hundred-dollar bill, although the end of the butt seems to be wearing a hole in the pit of his stomach. The sun is well above the tree-tops, and pouring down his rays without stint. He blinks to clear his eyes from hot mist, and looks at Jimmy, who still stands pole in hand.

"He's a big fellow, isn't he, Jimmy?" Jack inquires with a gasp.

"A whale."

"He's pulling now, I tell *you*. Did I do all right when he jumped?"

"You ought to lower your point the moment he starts to jump. If he should fall on your casting-line when it's taut, he'd snap it off short."

"He's twitching now; what does that mean? Tell me — tell me!" Jack cries, as the salmon begins to make a series of frantic tugs, which pulls the tip violently down, and then relaxes it.

Jimmy shakes his head ominously. "I don't like to see 'em do that."

"What does it signify?" asked Hasy.

"It's generally a sign they're not well hooked. He's trying to work the hook out of his mouth."

Jack trembles. The idea of losing him now is too terrible to contemplate.

"Give him all the butt he'll stand," says Jimmy.

"I'm doing it."

Once more the salmon is motionless. Only the strain and the perpetual thrumming tell he is there. Five minutes pass — ten minutes — and he never budges.

"He's sulking. Saw on him a little."

Jack saws, but without producing any impression.

"Step ashore and reel all you can, so as to draw him in slowly toward the canoe, and I'll try to get the gaff into him," continues Jimmy.

After some difficulty, owing to the necessity of walking backwards, Jack manages to clamber ashore, and to make a few steps up the bank, while the guide, having seized the gaff, creeps to the bow. By putting on a little more strain, Jack succeeds in reeling in a foot or two of line. It is wonderful to him to see how much strain his green-heart will stand. The tip is curved almost like a barrel-hoop. With all the might he dares to use, he endeavors to drag the fish toward Jimmy. The water is deep, and the current swift, however. The guide shakes his head again, evidently realizing that it is an undesirable spot for gaffing.

"Can't you reel a little more?"

"Look at my rod," says Jack; still he gives a fraction more butt.

Jimmy peers into the water, holding the gaff

just above the surface, ready to plunge it at a favorable opportunity. He tells Jack to move up river a step or two, and to slant the rod so that the line shall not come between him and the fish, in order to avoid entanglement with the gaff. There is a pause, during which Jimmy seems half a dozen times just on the point of striking; then suddenly he makes a strenuous dab.

"Missed him," he ejaculates, and simultaneously the frightened fish makes a desperate rush. Whir, whir, whir goes the reel, and Jack in an agony of dismay is forced to the water's edge. Again the salmon jumps, this time falling apparently flat on the line, but still he is on. Off he dashes. Whir, whir, whir, whir. He is just tearing.

"Get into the canoe," says Jimmy hastily.

"What's he going to do?"

"At this rate, he'll go over the rapid. We've got to follow him, if he does." So saying, Jimmy pushes off. "Sit down," he cries to Jack. But this is easier said than done, it seems to the young angler. With the butt planted against his stomach, he stands holding the rod as high up as he can, from which depends the long stretch of line separating him from his would-be victim, already on the edge of the foaming water which marks the beginning of the rapid some fifty yards ahead, and still making the reel fly. In front of Jack stands Jimmy, pole in hand; and behind sits Haseltine, grasping both sides of the canoe, and trembling with excitement. Yes, there is no help for it; the salmon is going over, and they must follow him. Already the canoe is moving swiftly. The whir of the reel has ceased, and there is very little strain on the line, which stretches from the tip of the rod to a point midway in the rapid like the rope which runs from the foremast of a vessel to the bowsprit. Where it touches the water, there is the salmon.

The danger now is of going too fast and overtaking the fish; and while Jimmy snubs the canoe, as he calls it, with his pole, Jack has to do some more active reeling. It is not very easy to keep one's balance in the midst of the choppy water, but Jack is afraid to divert his attention even so far as to try to sit down, lest he lose his precious fish.

The rapid was steep, and a couple of hundred

yards long, being caused by a series of rocks close to the surface, which transformed the current into foaming hillocks and furrows. Jimmy had to be constantly on his guard to prevent the canoe from striking, and once or twice they took in a little water over the bow. All the while the salmon was slowly forging ahead.

"Give him all the butt you can, so as to hold his mouth open," Jimmy kept saying. "He can't stand this long without drowning."

"I guess he must be well hooked, or he'd have been off before now," said Jack, as they neared the end of the rapid.

Here they came upon a stretch of still and rather shallow water, in which the salmon halted again, much to Jack's satisfaction, who was himself glad of another breathing spell.

"I must have had him on a good while," he observed reflectively.

"Two hours," said Hasy, looking at his watch. "It was three minutes of ten when you got him on, and it is just twelve."

"Whew! Do they usually take as long as that to land, Jimmy?"

"Not often," answered the guide with a grin. "The Colonel would have had him ashore an hour ago; but you're doing first-rate. Stick to him, and you'll come out all right. The world weren't made in a minute."

"How far would he run?" asked Hasy.

"If nothing breaks, he may get to the Basin before dark."

"Nonsense, Jimmy," said Jack with a laugh. "Oh, there he goes again, there he goes again!"

True enough the salmon seemed disposed to continue on his way down river. Whir went the reel, and out of the water he sprang once — twice.

"Let him go — let him go," cried Jimmy. "Don't try to check him too sudden. He's lively, and no mistake."

In spite of all that Jack could do, the fish ran slowly through the quiet stretch and reached another rapid. It was a short one, and below it was a dark pool. After reeling in the slack, there was still a good deal of line out, which showed that the water was deep.

"How does he feel?" asked Jimmy.

"Just as strong as ever."

"And how do you feel, — tuckered?"

"No," answered Jack stoutly. "That nasty tar oil will trickle into my mouth, though," he added, with a touch of despondency in his tone.

"You're not much to look at, Jack," said Hasy, laughing. "I'd say you were an Indian, if I met you in the woods."

Meantime Jack was feeling the salmon, who showed no disposition to move. Sawing proved again of no use. He was down in a deep hole, and declined to be dislodged by ordinary methods. Jack felt mortified and once more helpless. He said to himself that clearly he did not understand how to put on the proper strain or manage the rod cleverly. Instead of controlling the fish, he was himself dancing attendance on the good pleasure of his piscatorial highness. But what could he do? If he should exert more than a certain pressure, he might break the casting-line. Jerking would be equally dangerous. Jimmy suggested his stepping ashore and walking backwards again; but this did not help him much, for the salmon still stuck to the hole. He ventured to steady the rod with one hand, and to wipe the perspiration off his face with the other. In spite of his declaration to the contrary, he was beginning to feel fagged. Bah! he had forgotten the tar oil, and here was his handkerchief a mass of brown stickiness! Jimmy and Haseltine were laughing at him, too, as a consequence. It was confoundedly hot, too, and he was getting faint for want of something to eat. A sandwich would taste remarkably good.

This idea of luncheon grew upon him the longer the salmon persevered in inactivity, and took shape at last in a request for food.

Leaning up against a tree, he conveyed to his mouth with one hand bread and butter and potted tongue, while with the other he kept the point of his rod at a proper angle. Jimmy had built a fire and made himself a cup of tea, without which he declared that no meal was complete for him. After this refreshment, although there was no change in the status of the salmon, Jack felt much more disposed to take the initiative, even at the risk of losing the prize. This sulking must be put an end to somehow, and after consultation the expedient of hurling a large stone into the river close beside where the scaly brute was supposed to be was selected. The privilege of throwing the missile was claimed by Haseltine, who, standing by the water's edge, let fly.

The stone acted like magic. The salmon made a wild dash, excelling in impetuosity any he had hitherto indulged in, and, seeking the surface, leaped twice in quick succession. As he fell back the last time, Jack felt the line slacken, and cried bitterly, "He is off."

"No, he isn't," shouted Jimmy, and as he spoke the big fish leaped out of water right under their very noses close in shore, and a moment after still again beyond them up river.

"Let him go up," said Jimmy. "He'll kill himself against the current twice as quick."

But the salmon, thinking better of this plan, suddenly darted down again; and before many minutes the canoe was following him through a third rapid.

This passed, they reached another tranquil

shallow stretch; and here for the first time, as Jack tightened the line, the fish was visible near the surface, showing evident signs of fatigue, and now and then lolling over so that they saw the white of his belly.

"He's done for," said Jimmy.

Nevertheless, despite this assertion, the gamey creature presently gathered himself together, and made another smart rush toward the opposite bank. But Jack found it easy to check him now, and to guide him as he reeled him in, bringing him once more to the surface. Then Jimmy put Jack ashore on the sandy beach, which was a better place to land the fish than the bank where he had made the first attempt to gaff, and proceeded to wade out over his ankles. Jack had reeled in so that the casting-line was very near the ring of the tip. Accordingly, he had now to step backwards in order to pull the fish toward Jimmy, who cautioned him against reeling further. The salmon floated sluggishly, wagging his tail, and lolling more and more. As he caught sight of the gaff, however, he made still another struggle to escape, but only to be reeled back again the few feet that he had gained. Then he shook his head two or three times, and started to rub his gills against the bottom; but at this moment Jimmy extended the hook of the gaff across his back, and, dropping it into the water, drew it in with a quick motion, and lifted the silver beauty ashore.

"Hurrah," cried Jack, "hurrah, hurrah, hurrah!" and in a transport of delight he dropped his rod and cast himself on his knees beside the gasping fish.

Jimmy had picked up a stone to knock the salmon on the head, to prevent his wriggling back into his native element; but seeing him lying motionless he turned to the boys and said, laughing, —

"He's stone dead. You wore him out, Jack."

"I've got him, anyhow. Oh, I wouldn't have lost him for any thing! Isn't it splendid? O Hasy, I hope you'll catch one!"

"Tell him, Hasy, that the Colonel would say 'kill one,'" said Jimmy with a wink.

But Haseltine was too much carried away by the glorious result of the struggle to take advantage of the opportunity thus offered to revenge himself.

"Oh, what does he weigh?" was his fervent inquiry.

"Guess," said Jimmy, as he reached for the scales.

"I've no idea," said Jack. "He's a big fellow, though, isn't he?"

"I guess twenty pounds," said Haseltine.

"He'll pass thirty," said Jimmy.

"Really!" the boys exclaimed together.

The guide having inserted the hook of the scales in one of the salmon's gills lifted him from the ground. "What did I tell you?" he said. "Thirty? It's a good thirty-two."

"Hurrah!" cried Jack. "He's a buster. And how long was I in landing him?"

"Just five hours and four minutes," answered Haseltine.

"Five hours and four minutes! That'll make a great fish story," said Jimmy, bursting into laughter. "But it's true, all the same. It was nip and tuck between you, Jack. You wore him out, though, — may I never pole another stroke, if you didn't."

CHAPTER IV.

SETTLING DOWN.

WHILE Jack and Haseltine were thus busy down river, the home guard was by no means idle. It consisted, you will remember, besides Mr. Holt, of Dubsy Perkins, Max Fearing, and Tom Binney. There was Bingo, too, who was rejoicing quite as much as any of the others in the freedom of the woods. The lively fox terrier had come in the cart with George Coffin the day before, much to the dissatisfaction of his owner, who had wished to have him in the canoe; but the chances of his jumping overboard had seemed so considerable that Mr. Holt had issued a fiat compelling him to journey by land. Both he and his master Tom were in grand spirits this morning, being alike imbued apparently with the desire to ferret out something in the nature of bird, beast, or reptile from every suggestion of a hole in the ground or in the tree-trunks that met the watchful eye of either of them. And with some success, too, at least as far as Bingo was concerned; for the terrier, by dint of his keen smelling powers, hit upon the abodes of sundry chipmonks very early in the day.

"Seek him, Bingo, seek him," Tom would cry, as the little dog, barking vociferously, pawed at or sniffed before some significant orifice. But happily for the inmates, they were generally protected by the smallness of the holes from worse evils than a thorough shock to the nervous system.

Welcome as chipmonks would have been at home, here in the heart of the forest Tom's aspirations took a more ambitious form. Visions rose before him of deer and even bear trapped by his skill, and tamed by his discretion until they would follow his footsteps and feed out of his hand. But though these larger specimens were not likely to be run across in a ramble within ear-shot from camp, one might readily come upon a rabbit or an owl or a wasp's nest. As he very properly reasoned, one could never tell, until one looked, what was inside a hollow trunk or underneath a stone.

Either a woodpecker or a snake would be ample reward for any number of fruitless investigations. Therefore, whenever Tom's services were not required in other ways, he and Bingo went mousing round the neighborhood to see what they could find.

Dubsy, on the other hand, revealed great practical qualities. To chop wood, build up the fire, preside over the frying-pan, soup-kettle, and grid-iron, gather fresh hemlock for the bunks, or manufacture rustic chairs to make the camp more cosey, each and all seemed to him fascinating and highly desirable occupation. Mr. Holt, in perceiving this, was pleased. He had been anxious, as far as possible, to let the boys follow their respective bents, yet at the same time had intended that the drudgery of the camp should be performed by each in turn. But here was a boy with a genuine taste for cutting down trees, and broiling fish; who demurred neither at the heat of the fire, the dirtiness of the ashes, nor the stickiness of the pine-boughs; and whose sole grievance was that he was not allowed to do every thing in the domestic line himself. Clearly, if Dubsy preferred cooking to hunting for chipmonks, there seemed very little object in calling upon Tom to sacrifice the possibilities of meeting a bear, in order that he might do his share of camp work. The great thing was to have them enter heart and soul into something, and Mr. Holt felt that his duties were lightened by the fact that each of this pair knew what he wanted to do.

But poor Max Fearing had found the woods thus far not much of a paradise. Although the biggest of the six, he was inclined to be fat, and he was not strong in proportion to his size. His education abroad had separated him from other boys, so that he was unfamiliar with their ways, and he had never been accustomed to roughing it. Consequently his skin was very delicate, and his muscles limp from lack of vigorous exercise. To add to his discomfort, the black flies poisoned him, as they do some people, and his cheeks and eyelids were so swollen from bites that he could scarcely see. Of cooking he knew absolutely nothing, not even enough to set the kettle boiling; and contact with the raw materials, like butter, lard, fish-scales, or flour, incident to the preparation of food, disgusted him. In trying to slice a loaf of bread to make toast for luncheon, he cut his left hand, upset a teapot of hot water over one of his legs, and while gathering boughs filled his fingers with splinters. Yet in spite of all these ills, as they seemed to him, he made no complaints, bearing with equanimity and good humor the taunts cast at him by Tom and Dubsy on account of his awkward ways and what they considered his want of manliness. At heart, however, he was mortified. For his wounds, he cared little: they smarted, but far more painful was the discovery of his own deficiencies. Here he was a sort of Miss Nancy, with what Jack had called that morning "lady-like behavior;" and, moreover, he had not the least idea as to how he was to become like the rest of the boys. They could climb trees, talked knowingly already of poling and their ability to bake bread, and were keen for encounters with wild beasts; but he, Max Fielding, was utterly ignorant of all these matters, and would be apt to feel the inclination to run away at sight of a bear or wildcat. What use were books now? He *did* know something of *them*, and had a volume of poetry concealed in the rubber bag which contained his traps; but his principal dread was that it might be discovered by one of the others. As the sum and substance of it all, he felt very much like sitting down and crying; and the fear lest he might do so caused him to perambulate the camp with gritted teeth beneath a deceptive smile.

Mr. Holt, who was on the alert, was happily quick to perceive both Max's inability to cope with the others, and his determination not to give in. While the master believed that ridicule is a tolerably wholesome means of curing molly-coddled boys, and was therefore disposed to leave Max in a certain measure to his own reflections, he determined to aid and abet him in his efforts to make a man of himself. He noticed with satisfaction Max's good nature when jeered at, and the unflinching way he plunged his white hand into the butter-firkin during the lesson in breadmaking given him during the afternoon, although it was not difficult, for one used to reading character, to appreciate the boy's agony of mind.

About five o'clock Dubsy and Tom and Bingo were all so far tired out by the exertions of the day as to be disposed to squat down under a tree and remain comparatively passive. Mr. Holt took this opportunity to read aloud a book treating of the remarkable cleverness of ants, in the course of which Tom suddenly remarked, —

"I say, Max, did you ever see Bingo do arithmetic?"

"Really?" asked Max, who, having listened to the reading with absorbed attention, was in a receptive frame of mind.

"Why, certainly. He's great at it, especially at addition. Isn't he, Dubsy?" Tom added with a wink.

"I never saw his equal," Dubsy answered diplomatically.

"Come here, Bingo. Now, I want you to do a sum. Put down three, and carry one."

In obedience to his master's order, the terrier drew up one of his legs, and limped with gusto.

"There you have it," said Tom. "He put down three legs, and is carrying one." Whereupon he and Dubsy burst out laughing at Max's evident discomfiture.

"Max thought he would really do the sum in his head. Ho, ho!" was Dubsy's comment.

"Well, laugh away. I don't care," was the reply. But Max looked a little shamefaced.

"How could a dog do a sum? The trouble with you, Max, is that you're fresher than paint," observed Tom with the air of a sage. "I should think you'd be afraid of coming off on the bushes."

"Never mind, Max," said Mr. Holt. "These boys think they know everything; but I shouldn't be at all astonished if there were some surprises in store for them, before we break up camp. If I were going to make a prediction as to who would win the Colonel's rifle, I'm not sure that I shouldn't fix on you."

Max flushed and looked grateful. The expression of the other two was sardonic and evidently incredulous.

"You see," continued Mr. Holt, "because you

two are proficient at base-ball and rowing, and
have callous hands and hard muscles, you're
inclined to look down on any one of your own
age who can't say the same.   Now, Max and Joe
have been brought up in a different way; and,
though I'm not prepared to state that I don't
consider your way the better, I am very sure that
they would be able to put you to the blush in
more ways than one."

"Oh, Joe's all right!" said Dubsy with somewhat brutal frankness.

"I'm glad you approve of him; and let me tell
you that Max is all right too, so far that he is able
to talk French and German as well as his native
tongue, has a fine taste for music, and is remarkably clever at his books.   Those may not seem
very important acquirements in the woods here;
but they convince me that he has only to devote
his energies a little in another direction, in order
to become your equal as a woodsman.   I don't
mean to say," Mr. Holt added, looking at Max,
"that he is going to find it altogether easy to
overcome the timidity which I rather think he feels
in matters which a manly boy ought to take to as

a fish does to the water; but I am confident, that, if he keeps up his pluck, the day will soon arrive when you will not be able to stump him, as you boys call it, in many ways."

Tom and Dubsy, having listened in silence, continued to chew the cud of reflection while engaging in a game of stick-knife, which required no remarks, and was moreover a pastime calculated to awaken the envious admiration of Max. Just, however, as Tom had reached the interesting stage of holding the point of the blade on the crown of his head, preparatory to tossing the knife backwards, he was interrupted by a shout from Mr. Holt, who was looking towards the river.

"Canoe ahoy!"

Sure enough it was the Colonel. The boys rushed to the water's edge to peer into the canoe. But, sad to relate, there was nothing to be seen except one poor little pound trout, whose silver side had been dulled and parched by the sun. Old William had a disappointed look, and was shaking his head in a woeful manner.

"Where are your fish, Randolph?" asked Mr. Holt.

"Don't hit a man when he's down, my dear fellow. I've had only one rise this blessed day," answered the Colonel as he stepped out of the canoe.

"It beats anything I ever see," said old William, — "this time of year too."

"I've thrashed every pool as far up nearly as Mississippi, and tried every fly; but it was no use. The brutes wouldn't rise. There were plenty of them too."

"How do you account for it?" asked Mr. Holt.

"If you'll explain to me why salmon do rise on some days, I might be able to tell you why they don't on others. However, it's not the first time in my life I have come home skunked; and we must make the best of it. If an old sportsman such as I sets out to grumble, what can one expect of the rest of you?"

"But you're not wholly skunked: you've got the trout," said Tom, holding the parboiled fish up by the tail as he examined it with interest.

"True, I forgot the trout. That was Joe's handiwork. Come here, Joe," the Colonel said, nodding at the chunky little fellow, whose good-humored face had lost none of its cheerfulness in consequence of the day's ill luck. "Come here and tell these boys that if any one of them expects ever to be the owner of my rifle, he can't afford to leave you out of the reckoning."

"That's not unlike what I have been saying to them regarding his brother," said Mr. Holt, laying his hand on Max's shoulder.

"Ah!" said the Colonel, casting a scrutinizing glance at the elder Fearing. "All I can say is, as I said the other day, the best sportsman wins. And there's no greater mistake than to feel cock sure beforehand that this, that, or the other boy won't get it."

"Here comes the other canoe," broke in old William at this moment. "And may I never gaff another salmon, if the two lads are not poling," he added, as he shaded his eyes.

A moment later the canoe was in full sight, being propelled by Jack and Hasy, who, in spite of frequent splashing, were making slow but sure progress. It was five minutes before they were within hailing distance; and then the Colonel, making a trumpet of his hands, shouted, "Any luck?"

There was no answer.

"I guess they're skunked too," said Tom.

"W-h-a-t l-u-c-k?" It was Mr. Holt who holloaed this time.

But, though the inquiry must have been heard, those in the canoe saw fit not to make response. On they came, gaining inch by inch against the steep current, until at last old William had the canoe by the bow and held her fast.

"You don't say so!" exclaimed the Colonel, as he caught sight of the heap of alder bushes strewn over the bottom of the canoe. "How many?"

His inquiry was almost simultaneous with the murmur of congratulation and pleasure occasioned by Jimmy's removing the foliage with a proud sweep, and disclosing a brace of monsters.

"Well done, well done."

"Who caught them?"

"Hurrah! A salmon at last!"

"Two of them."

"But this one's a slink," said the Colonel,

completing the round of exclamations, as old William, lifting the fish separately from the canoe, laid them on the bank.

"'Him no bright salmon — him slink,' as Pete would say," responded Jimmy.

"That's a shame, Hasy," said Jack, breaking silence for the first time. "I hoped they wouldn't be able to tell the difference."

"Not tell a slink from a fresh-run fish?" exclaimed the Colonel with a laugh. "Thank you, youngster."

"It's too bad. Them slinks is a pesky nuisance," said old William.

"What *is* a slink?" asked Mr. Holt, expressing the general desire for information on the subject, which the four other boys were restrained by pride from putting into words.

"A slink is a salmon that's been in the river all winter, until he has become long and lean like this fellow. Don't you see how different he is from the other? Instead of being fat and shiny and full-bodied, he's shad-bellied and dark colored. Some call them black salmon or kelt," the Colonel added. "In the early summer they're apt to be a nuisance, as William says, for they're ravenous, and after being hooked are easy to kill. I've seen some of them make a pretty good fight, though. How was it with this one, Hasy, as I judge from Jack's words that he fell to your rod?"

"He had him on just half an hour by the watch," exclaimed Jimmy; "and, by the way he acted at first, I thought he was a bright salmon."

"Well, I don't see that there's much to complain of, then," said the Colonel. "And you killed the other one, Jack? He must weigh very nearly thirty pounds."

"Thirty-two," replied Jack with a pardonable air of triumph, and, inserting his fingers in the salmon's gills as he had seen the guide do, lifted him up for general inspection.

There was another murmur of applause.

"Isn't he a beauty? Bully for you, Jack," cried Dubsy.

"I'd like to have him stuffed," said Tom.

"How long did it take to land him?" asked Mr. Holt.

Jimmy snickered at this inquiry, and looked delighted.

"A good while," answered Jack, who, having found it impossible, even by the use of two hands, to hold up the fish for more than a moment, had laid him down again. "Five hours and four minutes."

"What!" exclaimed the Colonel.

"Gospel truth," said Jimmy.

"But what were you doing all the time, for goodness' sake? Five hours and four minutes? Impossible!"

"It was the salmon that was doing, not I. He sulked in a hole for two hours, and he jumped out of water twelve times. But I got him in the end, didn't I, Jimmy?"

Jack's enthusiasm was contagious, and he was plied with questions concerning the capture of his prize. The Colonel seemed immensely amused, and every now and then would ejaculate, "Five hours and four minutes! That's the best I ever heard!" and then burst out laughing. But no amount of merriment could have disturbed Jack's satisfaction. He was radiantly happy, and would gladly have recounted the details of the encounter so long as any one would listen to him. But Mr. Holt, insisting that he must be fairly worn out, sent him to his tent to get ready for supper.

In spite of having cooked during the greater part of the day, Dubsy claimed the honor of broiling the slices of the bright salmon that were served at the evening meal. The fish was in prime condition, and fairly melted in the mouths of the hungry sportsmen. Jack thought he had never tasted any thing so good in his life, though he was rather distressed at having the salmon used for food, as he would have liked to send it home to his mother. But there was nothing else except canned things for supper.

"We run across that fellow, Pete Labouisse," said Jimmy, in the course of conversation, after they had gathered round the fire late in the evening.

Old William growled. "No wonder the salmon won't rise," he said.

"He'd better not let me catch him lighting any flambeaux," said the Colonel. "Poor devil, I don't grudge his helping himself to a fish now and then, in order to keep soul and body together, but this wholesale spearing must be put a stop to."

"To whom do the salmon belong?" asked Max.

"It's rather difficult to answer that question in a single sentence," the Colonel replied. "Salmon are included under what the law calls '*feræ naturæ;*' that is to say, colloquially, creatures which are not tame; and therefore strictly they belong to no one. But being game and fit for food, the Government, here the Canadian Government, claims the right to regulate the manner in which they shall be taken, and to a certain extent who shall take them. Below tide-waters no one, except by express license, is allowed to net or otherwise capture salmon, and the same rule used to be until recently in force regarding the portion of the river above tide-waters; so that even if you or I owned all the land along the bank, and lived here from one year's end to the other, we should not have been permitted to cast a fly, on the ground that the Government had the right to make such laws as it chose regarding game. But a suit was brought a few years ago to test the question, and the Court decided that the Government had no power to prevent owners of land above where the tide flowed from fishing as much as they chose. But, unless one has the title to the land on both banks, it is permissible to fish only up to the middle of the stream, for that is as far as any one's property extends. Rather a lengthy explanation, Max, but I could scarcely put it into fewer words."

So passed the first day of camp-life. The following morning it was Mr. Holt's turn to fish; and he went down river, taking with him Max, while Dubsy and Tom went up to the Little Salmon Hole and the pools beyond, lying within three hours' poling distance from camp. The others stayed at home. The Colonel had requested George Coffin to send up an extra canoe, in order that the boys guarding camp might take lessons in poling and paddling.

The first day proved to be less satisfactory as regards the score made than any of the following seven. Mr. Holt, who, though no novice at trout-fishing, had never killed a salmon, came back with three beauties, captured at Miller's Landing, a pool below where Jack and Hasy had fished the day before, and having lost two others, — one owing to the breaking of the hook, occasioned by jumping, and the other through the rottenness of the casting-line. Max had hooked a famous fish, which had carried him half a mile down river, and finally broken the tip of his rod by running under the canoe. Tom and Dubsy also returned with one apiece. There was general rejoicing at so much good fortune, and every one declared salmon-fishing as a sport to be far in excess of his wildest anticipations. For the next week there was a continuation of the same luck. One day the Colonel killed five, averaging twenty-three pounds, one of which tipped the scales at thirty-four. With the exception of this last-named, there had been none caught so large as Jack's. By the end of ten days there was not one of the party who had not killed a salmon, and most of them could boast of two or three. Moreover, there was fine salmon-trout fishing, some of the trout running up to five pounds, — beautiful silvery fellows with red spots, — the same fish as the ordinary brook-trout, according to the Colonel, but modified in appearance by the influence of salt water and climate. How lively they were! The boys found it almost as much fun to fish for them as for salmon, if they used a very limber rod and light line. There were one or two rods among the collection that would bend at the slightest pressure, and they were greatly in demand.

"If you happen to hook a grilse with one of these, you'll have your hands full," said the Colonel the morning he produced them.

"What's a grilse?" three of the boys inquired at the same moment.

"A young salmon that has been to the salt water once. They run anywhere from three to eight pounds. I tell ·you, those fellows are lively."

It was not many days before several grilse were taken; and then the idea occurred to Jack, that the crowning feat in the piscatorial line would be to kill a big salmon with the lightest rod. Accordingly, one afternoon after lunch, while Mr. Holt was taking a siesta prior to resuming fishing, he pushed out in the canoe alone, under the semblance of casting for trout. It was at the Little Salmon Hole, and Jack selected the most likely spot in the pool. As it happened, the moment after his fly struck the water, he saw a swirl. Whir, whir, whir, whir, went the little reel, as if protesting by the shrillness of its tone against being employed to check such brute force.

"Cæsar's ghost!" muttered Jack, as the rod bent almost double under the feeble pressure which he ventured to put upon it. Out went the line at a terrific rate. There was only some fifty yards of it in all, and soon Jack saw that there was very little left on the reel. What should he do? What could he do? He looked toward the shore. Mr. Holt and old William were both still dozing.

Whir, whir, whir, whir, whir — snap! Then Jack realized that the tip of the delicate rod was dangling down in a shattered condition, and that the salmon was on his way to Gaspé Basin with all but a short piece of the Colonel's silk line. There had been one brief moment of extreme tension after the last inch of line had run out, and this was the result.

He had to listen to a lecture that evening. " Do you consider you acted like a sportsman, young man, in trying to land a thirty-pound fish with a twig of a tree and a skein of thread?" asked the Colonel. "Thought you could stop him? Nonsense! It was sheer bravado. You might as well have tried to kill a bear with a toy pistol."

The culprit hung his head. The taunt of un-sportsmanlike behavior nettled him; for he prided himself on being a thorough woodsman, and was determined that no one should outstrip him in the competition for the rifle. Yet here he had shown himself without doubt a silly fellow. Why had he yielded to the impulse? He had known well enough that the chances were ninety-nine out of a hundred he would not be able to check the salmon. He had not shown skill or ingenuity; he had simply been mischievous.

During these ten days the camp had been trans-formed into a veritable establishment. Chief among the improvements was a smoke-house, so called, — a hole in the ground filled with smouldering fire, surmounted by an arrangement of bark and boughs, in shape not unlike a circular tent, by means of which the smoke was confined. Smoked salmon such as one ordinarily buys from the grocer has been freely salted as well as dried, and is a very different affair from that treated to be eaten on the spot or within a comparatively short time. "Kippered" is the technical term, and a delicious adjunct it makes to the ordinary camp food. There was also a variety of benches, chairs, and tables, the result of experiments in carpentry by one or another of the boys. The lean-to for the guides had been enlarged to a log cabin, and from the flag-pole in front of the main house the stars and stripes flapped on the breeze. But what interested the six youthful spirits most was the pit which had been dug some three or four hundred yards from camp, and covered with boughs so as to produce the semblance of firm ground. Into this it was the hope of all, and especially of Tom, that some wild animal might tumble, in the course of trying to discover the meaning of so many signs of civilization in the heart of the forest.

Mr. Holt's plan was to remain about a fortnight

at Camp No. 1, and then to push on to the Big Salmon Hole, a day's journey either by water or by land, as there was a path through the woods, more or less blocked up by windfalls, but still that could be followed, leading up to it. At the Big Salmon Hole was another house, smaller, and not quite so comfortable as that below. Here the party was to pitch camp again; and after the pools in the vicinity had been exhausted, another five miles would bring them to the Narrows, as it was termed, a point where the river diminished materially in width, and flowed between towering precipices. Here also was the first stopping-place of the salmon in any considerable numbers, their farther progress up river being checked by a small cataract. According to the Colonel, hundreds of fish could be seen in the line of pools stretching below the fall by any one who looked down from the over-hanging trees when the water was low and clear. But many of the salmon, he said, chose their spawning-beds up farther, and after remaining at the Narrows for a while made nothing of ascending the fall. Night was the favorite time for them to attempt the leap, but it was no uncommon thing to see them by day-light climb up the roaring cascade by balancing themselves on their tails and swimming stoutly. Now and then a leap in the air, followed by a splash, told the story of mistaken aim; but it was only a question of perseverance when all who desired it reached in safety the upper pools lying at intervals along the ten or twelve miles which remained of the river before it was lost in a lake deeply buried in the woods.

One afternoon about the middle of the second week — it was the day before the Fourth of July, which was to be celebrated as became sons of independence — Joe Fearing, who was at Miller's Landing, happened to perceive a salmon within a few feet of the shore. He was standing on a sand beach where the water was clear, and the fish was so close to him that by moving forward a step he could have touched him with his hand. His first impulse was to call Dubsy Perkins, who with old William was getting lunch ready; then he thought what a fine thing it would be to haul the fish ashore unaided. The gaff was lying in the canoe near by: so he stole quietly away, and having supplied himself with the murderous weapon, which was very nearly as tall as he was, returned to the spot. The salmon was still there, comparatively motionless, and revealing life only by the slow vibration of his fins and tail. It seemed to Joe that here was an opportunity for distinction not to be neglected. To capture a salmon by main force ought to improve considerably his chances of being named the best sportsman of the party, and therefore of winning the rifle. So he reasoned; nor did it seem to him that he ought to abstain from wading the necessary steps because of not having on his rubber boots. Did old William or Jimmy ever hesitate to go up to their waists if there were occasion for it? And surely here was an occasion if there ever was one. Here at last was a chance to prove, that, though brought up abroad, he was no less enterprising and muscular than the other fellows. They should realize that only the opportunity had been lacking.

Joe had seen old William and Jimmy gaff salmon, and understood that it was important to let the hook sink well over the fish's back before drawing it toward him, so as to reach the spine. The salmon was a big one, not far from twenty-five pounds. Would he be very difficult to lift? Would he splash much? These were minor considerations, and not worth thinking about. How still he kept! Could he possibly be dead? Dead? Does a dead fish move his fins? Reassured by this reflection, Joe reached out, and after a pause jabbed the hook with all his strength into the salmon's side, and began to pull. He was up to his calves in the water, and the frantic struggles of the fish forced him forward in a moment up to his knees. There was such a terrific splashing, that his eyes were blinded. He had the monster on the surface, but it was all he could do with both hands to keep him there. The handle of the gaff seemed inconveniently long.

"Dubsy," he suddenly shouted, without exactly meaning to. "Du-b-sy!"

"O William, Joe's overboard!"

Such was Dubsy's agonized ejaculation. Startled by Joe's second cry, he had looked just in time to see his comrade, who seemed to be engaged in a terrible hand-to-hand encounter with something or somebody, lose his balance, and topple into the river.

"Into the canoe — quick!" exclaimed William.

What had happened? Joe was overboard indeed, and, despite his frantic struggles to recover himself, was being carried down stream by the current at a lively rate. For the first moment or two he seemed to be turning somersaults, and then some feet ahead appeared the handle of the gaff above the surface, bobbing in a wonderful way, and moving even still more rapidly than he.

"What has got him?" asked Dubsy, confident, apparently, that Joe had fallen prey to some huge river creature.

"Shove off," said William, without answering the question, and the canoe shot forward in pursuit.

Meanwhile, Joe's sensations may be said to have been mixed. Unable to pull the salmon out, or rather, while in the very throes of the tussle, his foot had slipped, and he had pitched forward. But conscious that his reputation was at stake, he had still retained his hold on the gaff. Then had followed a series of involuntary gymnastics on his part, performed midway between the surface and the bottom of the river, which ended somehow in his grasp being ruthlessly torn away. As blinded and gasping he rose above water, the instincts of self-preservation neutralized temporarily the bitterness of defeat, and he strove to gain a footing. For a moment he was unable to do this, for the river, though but moderately swift at this point, was deep. But, being able to swim, he did not lose his head, and almost immediately he was swept beyond the pool to where he felt his toes touch bottom. Twice he slipped on the stones and was submerged, but dragged himself ashore just before the canoe reached him. Then the smart of humiliation became superior to every other feeling, and in the hope of still redeeming himself, he cried to his would-be rescuers, —

"Where is he? Where is he?"

Old William, who had divined the situation and explained it to Dubsy, pointed ahead to the still bobbing gaff, and, sympathizing with the little fellow's desire to recapture if possible his late antagonist, shoved off the canoe with his pole, and followed after.

The frightened salmon, in his efforts to shake out the cruel hook, was dashing from one side of the river to the other.

"We'll get him yet," said Dubsy.

Only a few thrusts with the pole sufficed to send the canoe alongside of the struggling fish. After one or two ineffectual attempts to seize the handle of the gaff, William got hold of it at last, and amid a thundering splashing, which threatened to upset the canoe, lifted the salmon out of water, and dumped him inside.

"Hurrah," shouted Dubsy. "We've got him, Joe."

"Bully for you," was the grateful answer, and a few moments later the thoroughly soused salmon-spearer had the satisfaction of gazing upon his victim. Joe was fairly wringing with water, but his ardor was in no whit dampened.

"How much does he weigh?" he asked tremulously.

Dubsy produced the scales. "Twenty-six and a half," he said, as William held him up.

"Blind fish," observed William. "I thought as much."

Such was certainly the case. It was easy to see, on examination, that the salmon had lost the sight of both eyes. A sort of film was spread over each of them. Moreover, there were white streaks which looked sore in places about his head.

"He's been into the nets," said William. "He must have got caught in 'em, and was cut trying to get away."

"Poor fellow!" said Dubsy.

"That explains his letting me get so near him," said Joe. "I could almost touch him. I tell you he pulled, but I think I'd have got him ashore if my foot hadn't slipped."

"You look like a drownded rat," said William, breaking into a guffaw as he surveyed the dripping lad. "The best thing you can do is to pole for a spell, so as not to catch cold."

This seemed sensible; and Joe had just stepped into the bow, preparatory to heading the canoe for home, when old William added, —

"What you going to do with the fish?"

"Take him home, of course," Joe answered with evident surprise.

"Well, the dog'll eat him, I suppose."

"Bingo eat him? Not much. I intend to have him for supper to-night," answered Joe stoutly.

"Eat a blind salmon?"

"Why not?" the boys asked simultaneously.

"Joe Eden used to tell of how he'd been into the woods with a party that had seen a man die from eating blind salmon. I wouldn't take a bite of one for a fifty-dollar bill," answered the guide with deliberation.

Here was food for reflection, at any rate. "But I thought he got blind running into the nets," said Dubsy presently.

"He's been into the nets, it's easy to see from them white patches on his head; but maybe he got blinded there, and maybe not."

"He might have been sick," said Joe. "I don't think I'd be scared to eat him, anyway. Would you, Dubsy?"

"You might be dead men to-morrow," observed

old William impressively, "and I wouldn't bet a herring against it, neither."

It was difficult to answer such conviction as this, and a silence ensued which was scarcely broken until camp was reached. But so keen was Joe's satisfaction in his exploit, that the sight of Jimmy on the shore made him forget all but glory. He eagerly exclaimed, "I gaffed a live salmon. He pulled me overboard, but William saved him. He's blind in both eyes."

Jimmy cast a glance into the canoe.

"There ain't much luck in gaffing a blind salmon," was his comment. "Pretty moist you be, Joe."

This was scarcely an enthusiastic welcome. Indeed, so depressing was its influence, that before making any explanation of what had occurred, the two boys accosted Mr. Holt, who came up a moment later, with the questions,—

"Is blind salmon poisonous?"

"Would you eat blind salmon?"

The master naturally inquired why they wished to know. Thereupon, the adventure was set forth by them, and old William's observations repeated.

"Let's see the salmon," said Mr. Holt; so they went down to the water's edge and examined the fish, which had been left lying on the bank by the guides.

"He's a beauty to look at, certainly," continued Mr. Holt. "Wi-l-l-i-a-m!"

The guide approached.

"Please cut this fish open."

William did so. "Blind fish," he said.

"The flesh looks in first-rate condition. He lost his sight in the nets, I imagine."

Old William shook his head ominously. "Blind salmon no salmon. I didn't see him get blinded, sir."

"Well, you may cook him for supper to-night. If we are sick to-morrow, you'll be able to say, 'I told you so.' At any rate, we can't complain we were not warned," said Mr. Holt with a laugh.

But it was no laughing matter to William. He nodded vehemently as Dubsy remarked, "He says we may be all dead men to-morrow."

"Nonsense," answered the master. "That salmon is just as wholesome as any of those we have killed, you may depend upon it. We'll let him lie here until the Colonel returns, and see what he says."

Colonel Russell on his arrival half an hour later burst out laughing on being informed of the fears of William and Jimmy, and besides ordering the salmon to be served for supper insisted on eating heartily of it, in order that there need be no doubt as to its harmlessness. By and by, when they were sitting round the fire, he suddenly said to Joe, —

"I suppose you think you did a pretty smart thing to-day, young man?"

"Nothing extra," responded Joe modestly. Besides, there was a touch of sarcasm as it seemed to him in the Colonel's tone, that put him on his guard.

"At that rate, there'll be no chance for the rest of the boys. You'll get the rifle, sure."

There was no doubt now that the Colonel was being a little humorous at Joe's expense, but the other boys could not understand why. To them Joe's exploit seemed praiseworthy, and a decided feather in his cap.

Joe made no reply, and there was a pause before the Colonel said, —

"You and Pete Labouisse would make a pretty strong team. The fish don't get much chance when either of you are round."

"I didn't think there was any harm in it," faltered Joe.

"Pete would say the same thing."

"He showed pluck in holding on, at any rate," remarked Mr. Holt, observing Joe's unhappy expression.

"Pete also is apt to hold on to any thing he gets his spear into," said the Colonel with a laugh. "I don't wish to be hard on you, Joe; but, if you expect to be considered a sportsman, you must learn to give creatures some slight chance for life. I remember once seeing a man who was out gunning let a flock of birds sail past him without drawing trigger. 'Why in the name of all possessed didn't you fire?' I asked. 'I was waiting for them to light,' he answered. That man was too grasping. You certainly did show grit after you had gaffed the salmon, but I don't think you have any great reason to be proud of creeping up to a blind fish and giving him a death-blow. It's too much like stabbing a man in the dark."

"I didn't know he was blind."

"But you did your best to prevent his seeing you."

"Don't you think it's rather cruel to kill fish, anyway?" asked Haseltine.

At this question Mr. Holt chuckled slightly.

"There is a nut for you to crack, Randolph," he said.

"Yes, I appreciated that I was exposing myself to some such inquiry," responded the Colonel. "Your frank question, Hasy," he added, "deserves a frank answer; and mine is that, personally, I do not consider shooting birds and beasts and killing fish as cruel, provided the canons of sport are not disregarded. I suppose every humane man is conscious at times of feeling qualms while observing the struggles of a fish on the hook, and made to reflect that he is inflicting needless tor-ture. But, on the other hand, there is no denying that there are few things more adapted to make men healthy, vigorous, and manly, than hunting and fishing conducted in such a way that skill, energy, perseverance, and endurance are called largely into play. If one sees a partridge sitting on a tree and bangs away at him, or knocks him down with a stone or club, as I have seen men who called themselves sportsmen do, it is in my opinion animal murder, unless one is absolutely in need of food. Think, though, how many valuable qualities are put in training by legitimate hunting or fishing, — patience, alertness, courage, vigilance, good temper, and a host of others. It is their development, it seems to me, which justifies acts which viewed coldly by themselves might fairly be called cruel, and so unmanly. That is my view on the subject, Hasy."

CHAPTER V.

THE FOURTH OF JULY.

THE dawn of the glorious Fourth, which is heralded on all Yankee soil by the tooting of horns, and the bursting of Chinese crackers, broke calm and still. The party in camp was enjoying the sound refreshing slumber peculiar to those who have been all day in the open air. Doubtless, the younger spirits were dreaming of how the anniversary might be spent in the woods were there no check on the use of powder, for there had been whispered suggestions made the foregoing evening over the camp-fire, to the effect that the day must not pass without some appropriate demonstration. There had been a time, only a year or two before, when Jack Hall and Haseltine would have gloried in plotting to produce explosions. They had been members of a so-called "Big Four" at Dr. Meredith's school, a mysterious combination, whose offenses against order had resulted in the end rather disastrously for its members. Moreover, the two boys had been led, by the influence of the Doctor, to appreciate to some extent the error of their ways, and were therefore disposed to be cautious in originating or abetting mischief. But, as Tom had suggestively inquired, what objection could there be to waking up the woods a little? There were no neighbors whose property could be injured, and the wild creatures need scarcely be consulted.

It was this same Tom, who, just as the eastern horizon was becoming luminous, started up from his bunk and listened. Was not that Bingo barking, and barking excitedly? Tom reached forward and felt at the foot of his stretcher, where the little dog ordinarily slept, but he was not there. It was certainly Bingo. What could the matter be? He must have found something, and was waiting for his master to come.

"Hi there, Max," Tom said, in a hoarse whisper. "Do you hear Bingo?"

"What is it, Tom?" answered Max, in a bewildered fashion.

"Bingo's barking, and I'm going out to see what's up."

Tom was already out of bed and slipping on his clothes. "May be something has fallen into the trap," he continued. "I hope it's a bear."

"Are you going to call Jimmy?" asked Max.

"No, indeed."

"I guess I'll go too."

"Hurry up, then."

As Max threw off his blankets, he felt himself trembling all over. He had decided that if there was any chance of an encounter with a large animal, he ought not to miss it, and yet he did not exactly hanker for anything of the sort. He shivered a little as he thrust his bare feet into his boots, in response to Tom's suggestion not to mind his stockings, and put on his great-coat.

"Come on. Got your knife?"

Max had not. With fumbling fingers he drew it from the sheath of his belt-strap, which was hanging beside his head, and thus armed followed Tom outside. No one else was stirring, but Bingo was barking louder and more fiercely than ever.

"He must be close to the trap," said Tom.

It was barely light enough to see ahead when they were under cover of the trees. The pit was some three hundred yards from the limits of the camp, and the way to it was indicated by blaizes, which were difficult to distinguish at this early hour. But Tom simply went in the direction indicated by his dog's barking, pushing through the underbrush, and clambering over fallen trunks. Max followed close behind, trying not to mind the scratches, and rather fearful of stabbing himself with the bare knife.

"If there was anything in the trap, you wouldn't be able to distinguish it," he said, as he picked himself up after tripping on a root.

"That's a fact," said Tom, stopping short. "I guess I'll go back and get a lantern. You wait here."

"All right," answered Max. He spoke nonchalantly, but he would have preferred company. Tom had started off, and the only thing for him to do was to sit down on a fallen log and wait.

For a few moments he was kept in countenance by the sound of Tom's retreating movements; then there was nothing to break the stillness of the woods but Bingo's barking, which ceased only for sufficient intervals to let the little animal recover breath.

All of a sudden, however, he heard in front of him, but proceeding from a direction to one side of where the pit was, a crackling of twigs. Something was approaching. It could not be Bingo. The creature or creatures — for, judging by the noise, there might well be more than one — were moving slowly but steadily.

Max peered through the gloom. His heart beat very fast, and he felt an inclination to retreat. But that would never do. If it should turn out to be only a rabbit,— for Jack's experience had been made public by Haseltine, — he would be laughed at more than ever, and he was constantly being held up to ridicule on account of his inaptitude as a sportsman. Would it not be better to call Tom? No, Tom would be certain to return as soon as he could, at any rate, and a cry might well seem pusillanimous.

Here might be a chance at last to show himself to advantage.

Nearer and louder came the trampling, until he presently beheld what looked like a small Newfoundland dog appear from behind the nearest tree, snuffing the ground, and moving at a leisurely, waddling gait, — a circumstance which he did not especially notice, so relieved was he to find that the beast was only a puppy. But how in the world could a dog be here, and whose dog was it? While revolving these conundrums, Max plucked up courage so far as to murmur, —

" Poor fellow; nice fellow! Come here, sir."

But the animal thus apostrophized paid no attention; merely keeping on his way, which lay apparently off to one side of where Max was standing.

" Nice old doggy; pauvre petit chien," continued Max, in his efforts to be conciliatory.

Either because of the French or because he spoke louder, the beast stood still, and fixed his eyes on him.

" Nice fellow!" Max held out his hand.

But doggy was evidently not sociably inclined,

for he stood stupidly staring at Max out of eyes that struck him as strange looking. The guides had spoken of wild-cats. Were there wild dogs also, he wondered. Just then he heard Tom's welcome footsteps, and a moment later could perceive the glimmer of the approaching lantern. Bingo was still barking. The little terrier seemed not to enjoy the proximity of another of his kind.

"Max," uttered Tom in a deep whisper, having evidently suppressed his voice so as not to alarm whatever might be ahead, "are you there?"

"Yes; it's only a dog."

"Sugar! whose dog?"

"A Newfoundland pup."

"How do you know?" Tom exclaimed breathlessly, as he put one leg over the tree-trunk in front of which Max was standing.

"There he is." Max pointed with his knife-blade.

Tom looked, and for a moment gazed in a sort of brown study, then, with a repetition of the same whisper, but fifty-fold intensified, exclaimed,

"Newfoundland pup! Great Cæsar's ghost! it's a bear cub."

"Is it?" ejaculated Max.

Tom's eyes were fairly glowing with excitement as he stood for a moment reflecting on the situation. The idea had at once occurred to him of capturing the beast alive.

"I say, Max," he said, "you stay here, and I'll creep round behind so as to cut him off. If he starts forward, grab him."

"And put the knife into him?"

"Of course not. I tell you it's only a cub. Fling your coat over his head, if you're afraid of his biting you. He's a buster. Just the right size to tame."

"Oh!" said Max, beginning to understand.

The little bear, as if divining the stratagem, was showing signs of beating a retreat. Away went Tom, stealing circuitously. The victim suddenly hastened his movements, and disappeared from Max's view. Then there came various sounds indicative of a struggle.

"I've got him; I've got him," shouted Tom, but in such a tone as rather to convey the im-

pression to an unprejudiced listener that the
matter was not fully settled.

"Oh, oh! stop him, Max! Look out for
him."

These exclamations were almost simultaneous
with the re-appearance of the cub making straight
toward the other guard. It was no time for
hesitation. Remembering Tom's suggestion, Max
stripped off his overcoat, and, throwing it at
the creature, cast himself on top at full length
at the same moment.

"Good on your head," he heard Tom shriek
from behind, and he clung to the furry struggling mass with all his strength. But by this
time Tom was down beside him, and was holding
on too.

".Can you manage him alone for a minute?"
asked Tom.

"I guess so."

"Look out he doesn't nip you. He bit me
when I had him by the tail, and it hurt like
fury," continued Tom, drawing a cord from his
pocket, and watching his opportunity to slip a
noose round the cub's head. "Let him go now,

Max. He's all right," he added gleefully, when this was accomplished.

Despite his struggles, small Bruin was a prisoner.

"Hooray!" Tom cried with a jubilant caper. "Now, let's see what Bingo is barking at. Whoa, Emma!" he added to the struggling whelp. "You take the lantern, Max, and go ahead and see if there's anything in the pit, and I'll hold this fellow until you get back. Isn't he a beauty? What'll you sell him for?"

"He's yours, isn't he?" answered Max, looking puzzled.

"No; it was you who caught him. If it hadn't been for you, he'd have got away, sure pop," said Tom stoutly. "I suggested the overcoat, though, didn't I?"

"He's yours as much as mine. I should never have thought of stopping him but for you."

"Well," said Tom, "if you think it's fair, we'll go snacks on him. Won't it be fun training him? Hurry up now, and I'll wait here." He looked radiant.

Max, who was feeling pretty proud, picked up

the lantern, and marched on. Three or four minutes later there came a cry.

"Tom!"

"Holloa."

"Tom, Tom! Hurry up." There was consternation and excitement in the tone.

"I'm coming," Tom shouted. "Here you," he added to the cub; and then realizing that the bear would not budge, he ended by fastening the rope to a bough, and plunging ahead. Bingo was still barking, but much less vigorously.

"What is it?" Tom cried, as he came up,

Max was standing at the edge of the trap, the covering of which had been broken in; and Bingo stood beside him, railing evidently at something within. "There's another fellow in there. And, Tom, if you had been here just before I called, you'd have seen a bear, — a big one, I mean, — a monster," added Max, in an awe-struck tone.

"Where?" asked Tom with no less impressiveness.

"Right here. Close by the trap. He was on one side, and Bingo was barking at him on the other. The moment he saw me he got up on his hind legs.”

“ Really ? ”

“ Yes, and I thought he was going to run for me ; but he changed his mind, and got down again, and trotted off in that direction.”

“ How do you know it was a bear ? ” Perhaps remembrance of the Newfoundland pup prompted Tom to be incredulous.

“ Je le savais bien,” said Max with earnestness. “ He was just like those I have seen at menageries.”

“ If only you had had a gun ! ”

Max glanced at the bare knife which he still held. “ Would you have gone for him, Tom ? ” he asked with an anxious air.

“ A stab with the knife in a fatal spot would have finished him,” Tom answered with prompt indirectness. “ He might have hugged you, though, or knocked you senseless with a blow from his paw. They often kill hunters in that way, you know. But if you *had* happened to nail him, it would have given you a walk over for the rifle. I wonder where he is now. He may be close by still. It's probably a female, and the little ones are her cubs. This fellow's a dandy," continued Tom, holding up the lantern, and peering into the pit. In his excitement over Max's experience, he had almost ignored the second prize, but his interest was re-awakening. "He's bigger than the other. Now, we've each one."

After some further talk, the boys decided to leave the new captive where he was for the present, and to rouse the rest of the party. On the way back, number one was found safely tethered. Tom, having regained his hold on the cord, began his first lesson in discipline, and dragged young Bruin in triumph into camp. The only one stirring was Jimmy, who looked up from the fire he was building in astonishment.

"O Jimmy!" cried Tom, "we've seen a bear; that is, Max did. I was just too late. But he may be there still. You must get a rifle, and wake the Colonel."

"Seems to me you have him there," said the guide, as Tom paused in his excited address.

"He's a cub, and we've another in the trap.

Max thought he was a Newfoundland pup, and caught him by falling on top of him, after I had grabbed him by the tail and he had got away. He bit me, too, and left the marks of his teeth. But there's a big one, — the mother, I guess. Max'll show you the direction in which she went."

"What is all this?" cried a voice, and the Colonel's head appeared between the flaps of his tent. "Well, well," he added, as he perceived the cub, "you boys have done a fine morning's work already, I see. And you say there's a big fellow by the trap? I'll get my gun, and we'll look him up."

"I heard Bingo barking," said in his deliberate fashion old William, who had joined them, "but I thought he'd only treed another woodchuck. He's a regular babby. And you caught him all by yourselves, I want to know!"

"Step this way, Samivel, and let's have a look at you," said Jimmy, giving a playful jerk to the cord.

A few minutes later, the entire party was assembled; and, after rapturous inspection of the prize, all hands set off to extricate the other cub, and to try to discover the old bear. The Colonel and Mr. Holt had their rifles, and Jimmy carried an axe over his shoulder. On arriving at the spot, Jimmy jumped down into the pit, and after a slight tussle succeeded in tying a cord around the second cub's neck. The cub was then hauled up, and proved to be uninjured by his fall. He looked a trifle larger than his companion.

"Which do you want, Max?" asked Tom, anxious to have the question of ownership decided.

"I don't care. I'll give you first choice. Can we take them home?" he inquired doubtfully, glancing at Mr. Holt.

"You bet I'm going to take mine home," interposed Tom. "I've seen lots of tame bears. I can keep him in the stable at our country-place."

"We'll see," answered Mr. Holt judicially.

Tom selected, as his especial property, the cub that had been left at camp.

"Now tell us where the old bear disappeared,"

said the Colonel, turning to Max. "You're sure it wasn't a horse or a cow?"

This sally, suggestive of Max's mistake regarding the pup, made every one laugh.

"Never mind, Max," said Mr. Holt. "The Colonel is envious, that's all."

"It's no horse or cow that made these marks," said old William, calling attention to a series of footprints round about the pit.

The Colonel stooped to examine them. "Right you are; and you too, Max. He was a big fellow. It's only fair, my boy, to take you along with me, though it's not very likely we shall get a shot at him. Too many cooks spoil the broth: so if the rest of you expect bear-soup for your Fourth of July dinner, you had better go back to camp."

This seemed sensible, though disappointing. Accordingly, the rest of the hunting-party retraced their steps, Mr. Holt having kindly resigned his gun to the delighted Max, who, it must be confessed, handled it so awkwardly as to amuse the others. However, it was not to be denied that he had acquitted himself with credit

in the capture of the cub, and was, moreover,
the only one who could boast of having actually
seen the parent bear, so that he was decidedly
to be envied, even though they were able to
laugh at him. In the matter of guns, by the
way, the Colonel and Mr. Holt · had decided
before leaving home that it would scarcely be
prudent to allow six boys free use of fire-arms;
and thus the intention of several of them, to
come armed to the teeth, had been nipped in
the bud. Dubsy and Tom, who already owned
shot-guns, had been permitted to bring them;
but an armory had been straightway established
in one corner of the Colonel's tent, to which
they had been consigned. Pistols had been
entirely interdicted; and, indeed, the only death-
dealing weapon which the boys were at liberty
to bear perpetually about their persons were
their sheath-knives. As the chances of securing
many animals and birds were small, these precautions against shooting one another had seemed
advisable. But, on the other hand, Mr. Holt
was in the habit of granting leave to any one
or two of them to go off in search of game or

to fire at a mark. The result of the expeditions had been, up to this time, a few woodchucks, a rabbit, and an owl. The marksmanship of the party, however, had been materially improved by the target practice. Several of them, noticeably Haseltine, were able to pick off bottles at a considerable distance with great accuracy, and consequently confidence of hitting so large a surface as the body of a bear had been engendered. The Colonel had brought an excellent rifle and a breach-loading shot-gun with him, in addition to the prize-rifle, which was occasionally taken out of its case for general inspection, but was never fired.

On the way back to camp, after parting from the Colonel and Max, Tom asked for suggestions as to a name for his cub.

"You might call him 'Fourth of July,' in honor of the day," suggested Dubsy.

"Or Roderick Dhu," said Jack, who had a partiality for that hero.

Mr. Holt thought Castor and Pollux might be appropriate names for the pair.

Tom shook his head. None of the suggestions

satisfied him. "I guess," he said, "that I'll call him Dandy. I had a pony named Dandy once, and he died."

This pathetic reminiscence seemed an excellent excuse for the selection, if any were needed, and would have been gladly accepted by everybody, had not old William observed laconically that Tom's cub was a female. For a moment the owner's brow became clouded; then he exclaimed with some vivacity, —

"I'll raise cubs by her, then."

"You might," said William. "T'other one's a mate for her."

"If Max'll call his Dandy, I'll call mine Daisy," continued Tom, after a reflective pause.

All applauded this alliterative choice as highly appropriate. They had now reached camp, and the question was how to spend the day. It promised to be excessively hot, but Mr. Holt's proposal that they should go on a picnic to the St. John River, a five-mile tramp through the woods, met with favor. Jimmy was deputed as guide, and old William was left to guard camp. It seemed inexpedient to wait for the Colonel and

Max, as they had not returned when breakfast was finished; so, after being ferried across the river, they followed in Indian file the narrow path through the woods, which was really very little of a path after all, owing to the frequent windfalls, and the encroachment of shrubs and foliage. Before long they came upon an abundance of green moss, curious gnarled fantastic roots, huge toad-stools, and other fungus growths apt to be met with in a forest; and, with the morning's experience in mind, each of the boys was on the alert for game. Mr. Holt had yielded to the urgent request that Dubsy be allowed to carry his gun, merely remarking that the would-be hunter had better walk first in the file.

"Of course he should," Jack said with eagerness. "Otherwise the bear or the caribou might escape before Dubsy could get a shot."

"Ah, yes," drily responded Mr. Holt; "and he would not be so likely to shoot any one else!"

After they had gone about three miles, they came to a large lake. Just before reaching the edge of it, Dubsy, who was still in advance, stopped short, in consequence of a cautioning exclamation from Jimmy at his heels.

"What is it?" he whispered, as he squatted so that the tall reeds almost hid him from view, — a proceeding in which he was immediately imitated by the rest.

"Loons, — three of them. Right ahead."

By crawling on their hands and knees, the boys were enabled to get a little nearer, so as to obtain an excellent view of the birds without exposing themselves to be seen.

"They're a stunning shot, aren't they?" said Jack.

"How perky they look!" said Mr. Holt.

This was an excellent description of the loons' demeanor. Unconscious of danger, they sat comfortably on the tranquil water, proudly arching their long necks, or now and again protruding them with sudden energy to snap at insects on the surface.

Dubsy got his gun ready, and, recalling the Colonel's remarks as to being too grasping a sportsman, said tremulously, but with some discontent in his tone, —

"I'd better wait for them to fly, I suppose."

"If they will," responded Mr. Holt. "They're hard birds, though, to hit sitting, for they dive at the flash."

The loons were about one hundred yards off. They kept swimming slowly and without obvious purpose, but their general drift was rather away from shore. To Jimmy, who was accustomed to bag game in the most convenient manner, it seemed an unnecessary refinement not to fire at once ; but Mr. Holt preferred to let the seed of the Colonel's criticisms bear fruit.

"They're a drake and two hens," said Jimmy. "There's one way to start 'em," he remarked a moment later, as they took a decided slant in the opposite direction, "and that is to heave a rock among 'em. It may make 'em dive instead ; if so, there's an old scow yonder on the spit that we can follow 'em in. Be ready to blaze away the moment I let drive," Jimmy added, picking up a large stone and poising it above his shoulder.

The loons were now moving more rapidly, and keeping to the right, but parallel with the shore, which curved outwards on either side of where the party lay in ambush. To the left of the little bay thus formed, a strip of land well covered with underbrush, in the midst of which towered up a single large, overhanging tree, ran out into the water. This was the spit referred to by Jimmy, and the boys could plainly perceive one end of the scow protruding from the tall grass at the water's edge.

Jimmy threw back his arm, and hurled the stone forward. There was a vigorous splash, followed by a momentary flapping of wings, and then a loud report. This was almost immediately succeeded by another report, which proceeded from the spit of land. As the smoke cleared away, two of the loons were to be seen flying at full speed across the lake, but where was the third ?

" One's down," cried Jack.

" There he is, there he is," added Tom, pointing to a black object floating on the water.

" Yes, hurrah !" cried Dubsy, as he recovered his balance, which had been slightly disarranged.

But Mr. Holt and Jimmy, apparently uninterested in the result of Dubsy's shot, were staring blankly toward the spit of land over which the smoke of the second discharge still floated.

"It's that snake-in-the-grass Pete, I'll be bound," said Jimmy.

"What's the matter?" asked Jack.

"Didn't you hear the other shot?" said Mr. Holt.

It was the boys' turn to stare blankly now. So absorbed had they been in Dubsy's performance, they had not noticed it. All eyes were now directed toward the half-breed, who, in confirmation of Jimmy's words, rose at that moment from the tall grass in which he had been lying, and began to shove the flat-bottomed scow into the water.

"The black-hearted scoundrel!" ejaculated Jimmy, divining at once the Indian's purpose. "He's after that bird."

"But it's mine," cried Dubsy. "I shot it, didn't I, Jimmy?"

"Shot it? Of course, you shot it. I saw it fall with my own eyes. Say you there, Pete," he shouted, stepping forward so as to show himself, "that's our bird."

Pete looked up, and shook his head. He was in the boat, which was headed in the direction of the floating loon.

"Are you sure that Dubsy shot it?" asked Mr. Holt.

"Not a doubt of it. The skunk didn't fire until after the bird had dropped," exclaimed the guide in high dudgeon. "Here," he continued, turning to Dubsy, "give me that gun, and I'll drop him if he touches a feather."

"No, no," interposed Mr. Holt, "that won't do, Jimmy. It's our bird, I tell you," he shouted, in his turn, to Pete. "One of these boys killed it."

Again the half-breed shook his head. He was plainly steering straight for the bird, which was drifting away from him, and toward the shore. The boys were speechless with consternation and excitement.

"If I could only swim," cried Jimmy, shaking his fist as spoke, "I'd pull you out of your boat, and duck you in the lake, Pete Labouisse."

"I can swim," exclaimed Jack.

"Swimming is a happy thought," said Mr. Holt suddenly; and, as he spoke, he stripped off his coat, and began to free himself from his other garments. You are sure, Jimmy, that the loon is ours?"

"May I never draw another breath if it isn't!"

"Oh, what are you going to do?" cried several of the boys.

"Try to get there first. Perhaps it would be more sensible to let Pete have the bird, but it's a little too galling to see one's property carried off under one's very nose without an effort to save it."

By this time Mr. Holt was naked, and without delay he plunged into the water. The distance from the spit to the dead bird was some four hundred yards, of which the enemy had traversed about half. Mr. Holt had one hundred yards to swim.

"Go for him," cried Jimmy, who had an idea perhaps that the master purposed to carry out the programme that he had suggested.

Jack had stripped off his coat too, but a decided "one's enough" from Mr. Holt had suspended further proceedings on his part. On went the swimmer, launching forward, hand over hand; and simultaneously Pete, who had been taking matters easily, bent to his paddle.

Mr. Holt was a strong swimmer, but he had underestimated the swiftness with which his antagonist could propel even so clumsy a bark as the old scow. For a moment the struggle seemed from the shore tolerably even; but just as Mr. Holt was reaching out for the prize, the boat shot in between him and it, and his competitor, stooping quickly as he passed, snatched the dead loon out of water. For a moment Mr. Holt felt inclined to dispute the possession of the bird by seizing the nose of the scow, and if needs be upsetting her. But the victor, expecting perhaps some such manœuvre, sent his craft flying forwards by a series of deft strokes, then put her head to the shore, and the moment after she had touched the beach, picked up his gun, and disappeared in the thicket; turning his head at the last moment to utter a guttural note of triumph, and waving his dripping trophy above his head.

"I'd have sent a shot after him, if I'd been allowed," growled Jimmy, as he realized that Pete had won the day; though, as the gun was still unloaded, it may be doubted whether this bloodthirsty avowal was entirely sincere.

There was nothing for Mr. Holt to do, under the circumstances, but to swim back after the manner of the sometime king of France, who marched up the hill and then marched down again. Although worsted, he was feeling pleased on the whole that the affair had ended without a fray. A tussle in the water with a red man of the forest would scarcely have been consistent with his position as an instructor of youth, however satisfactory from the standpoint of adventure. Needless to say, his pupils were sorely disappointed, not only at the loss of the loon, which seemed to Dubsy serious, but at the humiliating termination of what had promised to be a thrilling encounter.

"Oh, why didn't you upset him?" exclaimed Jack, expressing the common sentiment of the five.

"He was too quick for me, Jack. You saw me make one grab for him, but it was no use. It is much better as it is, though. Supposing I had grappled with him, the dispute might have become very serious, involving great injury to one or both of us. And for what? Merely the possession of a dead duck, — which, after all, Pete may really suppose he shot. You see, if one thinks of it coolly, — and I am certainly able to now," he said, as he wrung the water from his fingers, "though I admit that the bath was refreshing, — there was certainly not much worth fighting for. I was led away, as we are all apt to be, by the indignation of the moment."

"But the principle was the same," said Jack with a martial air.

"Yes. I suppose that is so," replied Mr. Holt, smiling. "We may fairly submit, however, without serious loss of dignity, it seems to me, to have one's rights trampled on to such a limited extent. I'm aware that it is the Fourth of July, and that all of us except Jimmy are free-born Americans; and yet, nothwithstanding, I do not feel disappointed that I did not get my fingers on Pete."

The boys found difficulty in accepting this rational view of the matter, and they had a firm abettor in Jimmy, whose muttered denunciation of the half-breed boded ill for the future welfare of that worthy. Mr. Holt having dressed himself, the line of march was taken up again. The heat had increased materially, and though the foliage protected them from the glare of the sun, the air was dense and oppressive.

"It wouldn't surprise me if we got a thunder-shower before night," said Jimmy, squinting at the sky.

On reaching the camp at the St. John, where there was a cabin similar to their own, every one was ready for lunch, which was devoured with avidity. After this, Mr. Holt, who had brought his rod, set out to try such of the nearest pools as could be fished from the shore. The boys expressed delight at the transparence of the water, which, unlike that of the York, was in many places clear as crystal, and of an apparent greenish hue, induced by the color of the stone bottom. But, though there were fish to be seen, not even a trout would rise. Jimmy declared that it was useless to cast during such heat. The salmon seemed scarcely to notice the fly as it sailed down over their noses. By climbing a tree overhanging one of the pools, a bevy of them were to be seen resting in small detachments a few inches from the bottom, wagging their tails indolently. Once in a while, a fellow would cock one eye up, as though slightly interested; and there was a solitary fish at the farthest end of the pool, who, after taking notice in this manner a number of times, displayed curiosity so far as to swim half-way to the surface. But he either became disenchanted, or the exertion proved too burdensome; for he languidly turned tail, and whisked back to his former station, from which nothing was able thereafter to allure him. Mr. Holt became convinced at last that he might as well be casting over empty pools, and took apart his rod.

"There'll be great fishing after we get a shower to freshen up the pool a bit," said Jimmy.

As this could prove advantageous only to the anglers to whom St. John belonged, and who were expected to arrive on the morrow, the boys were but little cheered by the announcement.

As it seemed more sensible to wait until the sun was lower in the heavens before retracing their steps, a spot as shady as possible was selected as a shelter. Here both Mr. Holt and Jimmy, with a view to comfort, stretched themselves out. and speedily fell asleep. But to the junior portion of the party, the idea of slumber in the daytime, and especially on the Fourth of July, seemed an impious waste of time. To tell the truth, they felt rather restless. What with the associations awakened by the day, and the adventure with the loon, their faculties were on the alert, so to speak. There was a certain reflective gravity in their individual expressions as they sat around, which would have put one accustomed to observe youthful physiognomy on his guard.

"Of course they don't think much of the Fourth of July here," said Jack, breaking a spell of silence, jerking, as he spoke, a pebble into the water.

"Jimmy didn't know anything about it. He'd never heard of the day," observed Haseltine.

"I believe, though, that an American ought to

celebrate it just the same when he's away from home, don't you?" continued Jack. "Patriotism oughtn't to depend merely on where you happen to be."

"That's so," said Dubsy emphatically.

"But what can a fellow do?" inquired Tom, giving a less impersonal turn to the conversation. "We haven't got fire-crackers or rockets or a tar-barrel, and the only powder we have is in Dubsy's cartridges. It's a poor lookout, so far as I can see."

"There's one thing we might do," said Jack. "It wouldn't amount to much, but it would be better'n nothing."

"What's that?" asked several together.

"Build a bonfire. What would be the harm?" he added, to disarm criticism.

"None that I know of," said Hasy, casting a glance at the sleepers. "There's an axe up at the camp: so it wouldn't take long to get enough old stumps together to start her with."

"Let's have a big one while we're about it," said Jack, rising to lead the way up to the cabin, a few hundred yards distant. Confident as they professed to be that there could be no objection to the plan, there was no unnecessary noise made in taking their departure. In fact, an unprejudiced observer might have said that they slipped away.

There was plenty of good material at hand, —dried underbrush, and decayed trunks that yielded to the first strokes of the axe; and in a few minutes they had erected an impressive pile.

"Seems to me I smell smoke already," said Haseltine, sniffing the air, as a lighted match was being applied by the patriot Jack.

But his remark failed to interest the group, whose entire interest was centered, for the time being, on the bonfire, which speedily became splendid with crackling flames. Five diligent boys, with a forest at their back, were surely qualified to produce a grand conflagration. They had, however, pitched it in a comparatively clear spot, so as to confine it within moderate bounds. They could certainly boast of a success; and, as they stood watching the blaze, the only drawback seemed to them to be a lack of spectators. Mr. Holt and Jimmy were too sound sleepers. Why did they not wake up? And yet no one of the boys saw fit to rouse them. Assuredly either would be glad to forego the remainder of his nap to behold such a splendid sight. Why did no one see fit to give them the opportunity? They could not possibly object; at any rate, it would be useless to do so now. Besides, they would have to know sooner or later what had been going on. This seemed indisputable reasoning, and yet no one stirred. Could it be, that, though the boys had selected the safest spot for their bonfire, there was a secret hope in the hearts of each of them that it might spread, in spite of their most strenuous efforts, so as to include at least a copse or two of trees, or an acre of underbrush? If this were the case, each of the conspirators, nevertheless, conscientiously stamped out each indication of extending which the stealthy element displayed by creeping along the grass. If they were buoyed by any such hope, each kept it to himself, and gave no sign. Still they were preternaturally grave.

In the glade below, one of the sleepers stirred at last and woke, — woke, and, sniffing the air suspiciously, sprang to his feet. It was Jimmy.

"The woods are on fire!" he ejaculated; then, as he caught sight of the column of smoke ascending from the bonfire, added, "Humph! It's them boys."

His exclamations served to awaken Mr. Holt, who, rousing himself, inquired sleepily, "What's that you are saying, Jimmy?"

"They've made a big fire up to the camp. Pesky dangerous this time of year, when everything's so dry," answered the guide, looking back over his shoulder.

The master followed. Although the blaze was prodigious, there were no serious indications of it's spreading; and Jimmy had to content himself with grumbling a little, and keeping a watchful eye on the grass. It was certainly a fine sight, and the satisfaction of the boys was now tolerably complete. Any hope they might have entertained that the woods would catch had been too remote to mar their serenity.

"Pesky dangerous, though," muttered Jimmy from time to time. And Mr. Holt, in more specific language, called attention to the risks of building so huge a fire in the present parched condition of the underbrush.

"We were very careful," answered Jack; "and it didn't seem right that the Fourth should pass without some sort of celebration."

A good half-hour elapsed before the fire exhausted itself after they had ceased to heap on fuel. Jimmy declared that he wished to see the embers quenched before setting out for home: otherwise, a wind might arise and scatter them. The effect of the conflagration had naturally been to make them all even hotter than before, which was saying a great deal, and, moreover, the air seemed to be impregnated with the aroma of burnt logs. This odor did not diminish after they had begun to retrace their steps, which evidently struck Jimmy as strange; for when they had proceeded half a mile, and it was still noticeable, he snuffed the air two or three times vigorously.

"Why do you snort like that?" asked Hasy, who was next behind.

"I don't understand it," said the guide, without paying heed to the question. "Whatever wind there is, is dead ahead. I should say from the smell there was a fire burning here somewhere."

"Perhaps it's Pete cooking his dinner," said Dubsy.

"Pete's up to no good, whatever he's doing, you may be sure of that," Jimmy replied, by way of answer.

On they went in silence for about a mile, while the smell of burning wood grew more and more distinct. There seemed to be a sort of haze in the atmosphere. Jimmy sniffed no more; but he kept inciting Dubsy, by keeping close at his heels, to travel at a lively pace.

"Here, you'd better let me take that gun. It's too heavy," exclaimed the guide at length, reaching out and seizing the barrel.

"No, no; I'll take it. I'm not tired."

"Step along, then. Don't waste time talking."

"What's your hurry, Jimmy?"

"You won't have much chance to talk about hurrying, if the fire catches us."

"The fire?"

"Yes; the woods are on fire."

As he spoke, Jimmy stopped, and waiting for Mr. Holt to come up repeated the announcement.

"The woods are on fire ahead."

"Ahead?"

"Yes; and it's my belief that Pete Labouisse could tell who set 'em. There's no time to be lost if we expect to get to the river. This is no place for a lame man."

"Moses!" ejaculated Hasy, as an outlet for his emotion.

Mr. Holt looked grave. "If the fire is across the path, there'll be no use trying. We'd better turn back."

"It's six of one and half a dozen of t'other, according to my figuring, whether we turn back or keep on," answered Jimmy. "The smoke seems to be coming from there," he said, pointing at an angle about half-way between the path ahead and the extreme right; "and with the wind in our faces it's sure to gain on us if we turn, and we may get round it by keeping on. It's the same distance either way."

His speaking of smoke caused them to look up. Above the tree-tops the murky haze was more perceptible, and made the sky look dingy. There was no time for indecision.

"Whatever you say, Jimmy. You know best. Remember, though, these boys are under my care."

"Keep on, then. But you. must run for all you're worth," the guide said, sweeping his glance around the youthful group. "I'll lead the way."

Instinctively the boys girded their loins by tightening their belt-straps, and as Jimmy darted off with the gun over his shoulder, which Dubsy had given up in response to a second demand for it, followed as best they could in single file the swinging pace set by the leader. Mr. Holt brought up the rear. The heat was forgotten, oppressive as it was. Now the chief concern was to clear at a bound fallen trees, and to guard one's footing against the roots and other impediments in the path. There were about two miles between them and the river.

Presently a sudden breeze fanned the foliage, bringing a denser quality of smoke into their faces. The tree-tops swayed, and Jimmy, turning, exclaimed, —

"The wind's rising and shifting in our favor!"

A few minutes later this became obvious; although still in front of them the draught was blowing now more from the left of the path, tending to keep back the conflagration which was on the right-hand side. Almost a gale seemed to have taken the place of the sultry calm. The odor of the burning forest had become pungent and rasped the throat. Then, as they reached a portion of the path where the growth was but moderately thick, a blaze met their view in the near distance. A wall of fire, the crackle and roar of which startled them into renewed energy, rose like a huge wave threatening to ingulf them. Simultaneously, the cries of animals and birds were audible. Three caribou, a doe, and two fawns, lashed by fear, plunged madly across the path between Jack and Hasy, causing them to utter expressions of bewildered regret at the loss of such an opportunity, which even the seriousness of the situation could not check.

On the party tore, individual members now and again pitching headlong or rolling over, but righted as often as needs be by the rear guard, who well might feel anxious at so perilous an experience. Nearer and nearer the wave of flame was creeping, so near that the tossing branches

seemed to be fiery arms stretching out to snatch
at them.   They could feel its heat, and the smoke
choked them.   At last Jimmy gave a warning cry,
and turned sharply from the left out of the path.
Those behind perceived that a large tree bordering
it was already in flames.   The path was no longer
free, and they had now to plunge along, fighting
their way through brake and bramble.   The
master held Joe's hand.   The little fellow's
plumpness made so long a run exhausting.   The
others dashed ahead as best they could.

"Only a little farther," shouted Jimmy.   "We
shall soon be there."

"Run, boys, run," Mr. Holt cried, spurring them
on from behind.

The whole forest seemed alive with the jabber
and screams of the frightened denizens.

"Hear the bears howl," said Jack to Tom, as
they forged along abreast.

"It's awful," was the answer, expressing the
young trapper's sense of the whole situation.

Just then Jimmy shouted at the top of his
lungs,—

"Holloa-a-a!   Holloa-a-a!"

THERE SEEMED TO BE A RING OF FIRE AROUND THEM. — P. 193.

Almost immediately there came a similar cry in response, which seemed to proceed from close at hand.

"Thank God!" ejaculated Mr. Holt.

"It's the Colonel," said Jack.

Again Jimmy darted aside. The underbrush beneath his feet was crackling, and dense black smoke was pouring around him.

"Keep together," he shouted excitedly. "Holloa-a-a!"

"Holloa-a-a!" came the answer back.

They were close to the river now. That was certain.

"Oh, oh!" ejaculated Hasy and Jack at the same moment, as a fringe of fire fell down upon them from a blazing birch. But, though scorched, they managed to shake off the brands.

"My feet," cried Joe, hopping in pain.

"Steady, my boy. Be brave a moment more," said Mr. Holt.

There seemed to be a ring of fire around them. Jack seeing Dubsy pitch headlong at this moment believed their last hour had come. Then followed a vigorous shout. He saw his friend lifted up and dragged forward, and felt himself grasped by strong arms. That was all he knew until he opened his eyes and became aware that he was in a canoe. Before him sat Colonel Russell, black as an Indian with smoke, and minus some of his beard and his eye-brows, paddling. Beyond, as far as he could see, the woods were buried in smoke and flame.

The Colonel nodded encouragingly.

"Where's Dubsy?" asked Jack, half raising himself.

"Sit still. He's safe. You're all safe. But it was a terribly close call."

Jack shut his eyes again, and sank back exhausted. His throat felt like molten lead, and his eyes parched. Beside him, in a similar condition, lay Tom and Joe. Jimmy was in the bow, still grasping Dubsy's gun with hands from which the skin was off in many places. Old William was convoying the rest of the party; and in a few moments they were all reassembled on their own side of the river, none the worse for their hazardous experience beyond a few burns, painful, but not important.

The spectacle they now beheld was most impressive. The dusk was coming on apace, and the whole forest, so far as the eye could reach, was wrapped in a blaze of glory, lighting up the sky and hills obscured by the approach of night. The carnival of creature sounds had increased, and the cries of fright and dismay were answered by sympathizing notes from across the river.

"You never saw such fireworks as that, boys," said the Colonel. "It beats any Fourth of July show that any of us will ever see."

"I'm glad we didn't set it, though," said Jack a moment after, reflecting doubtless on what might have been.

"And if it ain't murder that Pete ought to be tried for, it's something mighty close to it," observed Jimmy.

"There's no evidence that Pete set the fire," answered the Colonel.

"I guess he done it all the same," said old William slowly.

There was not enough confidence in any one's mind that the half-breed had not been concerned in the matter to induce further opposition to the view taken by the guides. The Colonel contented himself by remarking that it was not wise to jump at conclusions without sufficient data, and then called attention to the heavy cloud overhead rapidly overspreading the illumined sky.

"A thunder-storm," said Jimmy.

Just then a streak of lightning ran zigzag through its midst, followed after an interval by a deafening peal, that rumbled among the hills, and came echoing back. At the sound, the energies of the beasts and birds, which had become more quiescent, burst forth in redoubled volume. Even Dandy and Daisy lifted their voices in unison with the universal wail.

The huge black cloud as it advanced grew molten with the vivid reflection of the sea of flame beneath. Twice and thrice the thunder-bolts leaped from it, as though eager to unite with their kin, and the earth trembled with the uproar. Then came the rain ; at first in large single drops, then fast and faster, until it poured a deluge.

"That's the talk," said old William with satisfaction. "The woods won't burn long if that keeps up."

His words were cut short by a flash and a tremendous clap that made the boys fairly jump. It seemed as though the bolt must have struck within a few yards of the shanty, so soon did the report follow the lightning. After it came wind in violent gusts, and floods of water. The cabin was the only shelter; for, though the tents might be waterproof, there was no certainty that they would not be blown down by the fast rising tornado. For hours the rain fell in torrents, and the thunder crashed about their ears. Through the window they could see the glow of the fiercely burning conflagration gradually fade in intensity, until at last at midnight, when the storm had moderated, there was only a faint glimmer in the sky. A gentle drizzle was still falling, which promised to quench the last flicker before morning. On inspection prior to turning in, a tree about a hundred yards from camp was found to have been struck and splintered by lightning, and the tent occupied by Max and Tom had been overturned by the wind. Altogether it had been a day of adventure, and as much out of the ordinary run of days as a Fourth of July at home. All were weary, and the soles of Tom's feet were decidedly painful. His roommate Max felt likewise foot-sore. He had tramped most of the day in pursuit of Mama Bruin, but without seeing more than her tracks, which had vanished at last.

CHAPTER VI.

AT THE BIG SALMON HOLE.

NEXT morning, although the sky was clear and fine, an expanse of gray smoke overhung the hills; and across the river, as far as the eye could penetrate, a melancholy vista of charred and blackened stumps was disclosed. It seemed a fitting time to change the scene; and immediately after breakfast camp was broken, and the canoes were laden for the expedition to the Big Salmon Hole. The spirits of all were somewhat dampened, however, by the fact that old William and Jimmy were not to be of the party. The Colonel and Mr. Holt had come to the conclusion that the services of the guides were no longer necessary, and that the boys would become better sportsmen by being obliged to depend upon their own exertions.

The Big Salmon Hole was distant a full day's

journey in the canoes. As the guides predicted that the rapids would be getting shoal, on account of the fall of the water during the last few days, it was important to dispense with all luggage not absolutely indispensable to comfort.

"You boys will have a chance now to rough it a little, and to understand what life in the woods really is," said Colonel Russell, who seemed to feel more than commonly good-humored at the idea. "You've been feasting on the fat of the land down here; but where we're going to you'll get no fresh butter, bread, eggs, and cream, I can tell you. After this it'll be salt pork for breakfast, salt pork for dinner, salt pork for supper."

"That doesn't frighten us a mite," said Jack nonchalantly.

The only bones of contention were the cubs. The idea of parting with them was too painful to be entertained by the boys without remonstrance, and after much argument passports were obtained for the youthful Bruins. By half-past nine all was ready, and the Colonel and Mr. Holt led the way in the first canoe, which was freighted with the heavier portion of the luggage. Then came Max, Hasy, Joe, and Dandy, and bringing up the rear the other three, Daisy, and Bingo.

"Good-by, William. Good-by, Jimmy."

"Good-by and good luck, and I hope you'll come down with your gunwales under water 'cause of the fish," cried the younger guide, in reply to the chorus of farewell shouts, while old William grinned, and waved his hat. Then the iron sockets clattered against the bottom, and the crews were off. Jack stood poling in the bow of his canoe, and Tom in the stern; while Max and Hasy filled the corresponding positions in the canoe ahead. The other two boys had made a pillow of Daisy and Dandy respectively, and were comfortable.

Thus far the party could boast of fine sport. In the past fortnight, forty-two salmon had been taken, averaging twenty-three pounds; twenty more had been played, but lost, owing to a variety of mishaps. This one had wriggled off the gaff; the hook had worked out of another's mouth just as he was ready to be landed; a third had twisted the casting line around a snag, and broken it; in the case of a fourth, the head of the fly had parted without apparent reason; and a fifth, — so one might go on through the category. It is better to record the simple fact that in each case the fish got away, leaving the unfortunate angler to experience, as he felt his line relax, that terrible sinking sensation in the pit of the stomach, which only those who have lost a salmon can perfectly realize.

Now they were going still farther into the wilderness in pursuit of the fish that had pushed on to the pools near the head of the river. The fresh air and invigorating exercise had tanned the complexions of all, and given to every one of the six boys a greater appearance of robustness. Mr. Holt, as he looked back at the youthful strugglers against the current, smiled with satisfaction at so many evidences of the benefit already worked by their outing. Nor did he believe that the benefit was merely physical. Can the mind of an energetic, full-blooded boy of sixteen fail to be quickened and stirred and interested by the beauty of unredeemed nature?

While he is breathing into his lungs the pure atmosphere of the woods and mountains, does not his heart thrill at moments with a keener sense of living, realize the exalting consciousness that life should be broad not cramped, pure not defiled? As he feasts his eyes on the sparkling, foaming water-course winding out from stately hills, whose slopes reflect in turn the majesty of dawn, noon's luxuriance, and the reverie-begetting shadows of the evening hour, does not his inner vision now and then catch glimpses of life's deeper meanings, which bring the queries to his lips, " What am I doing? What is the purpose of my days?" There is nothing like severing completely for a time one's relations with human beings as they ordinarily live, in order to escape from ruts, and readjust one's perspective. Those of us who are grown up realize this; and though the hobble-de-hoy of sixteen, either from false shame or some kindred cause, may be less willing to admit his suscepti-bility to Nature's influences, you may feel certain that nine times in ten (I could almost say ninety-nine out of one hundred), the poet in him — what

Will Shakspeare calls the part of his mother that every man has in himself — is all awake and quivering. While he seems to be caring merely for killing more fish or shooting more birds than any one else, do not take it for granted that he is not making good resolutions as to what he will do when he gets home. There is many a boy who has returned at the beginning of the new school year a metamorphosed being. He was indifferent once, listless, mischievous, a mere hand-to-mouth sort of living lad. Now he is alert, eager, ambitious, with eyes that tell of some new power at work within him. We all know what that means; the man in him is awakened. But if you seek the cause which has wrought the change, which has kindled the sacred fire, many a time you will find that the trees and the water-falls and the birds and the presence of the ever varying hills have had their share in it. Nature is God's best interpreter.

Jack's canoe had been the last to get away, and almost immediately the consciousness that the others were ahead became disagreeable to him. Boating was a specialty of Jack's. Already he was one of the best oars at Utopia School, and he had made up his mind long ago that before graduation he would become its champion; therefore it nettled him to see so inferior a crew as he set down Max and Hasy to be in the lead. Accordingly he proposed to pass them; and he hoped, after doing so, to be able at least to press the Colonel and Mr. Holt also. He said nothing to Tom, but gave a series of vicious shoves with his pole, that sent the canoe flying forwards. A moment later its bow almost lapped the stern of the one in front. Max and Hasy turned their heads, and Joe, who assumed, perhaps, that because he was doing nothing, he was captain, saw fit to remark, —

"Now, don't waste your energies in trying to pass us, Jack, for you can't."

As Joe finished speaking, his crew, evidently seized by a determination not to renounce the lead without a struggle, bore energetically upon their poles. They had just reached the foot of the first rapid, and now ensued much clattering caused by the contact of the iron sockets against the rocks in the river; and not only clattering, but spattering also. The canoes swayed and wobbled; and Jack and Max respectively, in their positions at the bow, found difficulty in not falling overboard. I can tell you, boys, poling against the rough waters of a salmon river is no child's play; and if you hurry, you are pretty sure to come to grief in one way or another. Before they had proceeded more than a hundred yards on the rapid, each of the two bow-oars — if we may so style them — was forced to the conclusion, that, unless he moderated his efforts, the water would be soon pouring into his canoe through a hole in her side. Bumpety, bumpety, bump, was the not exactly pleasant music that rung in their ears at every attempt to force the pace. Evidently, to make headway, the path must be picked with deliberation.

This irked Jack, who would fain have shown the superiority of his biceps by a continuation of the savage pushes in which he had indulged at the start; but he saw that he must control his ardor if he hoped to win, to say nothing of not smashing the canoe, against which he had been cautioned in express terms by the Colonel just before leaving camp. The only course to adopt at the moment was to tag on behind the other, and wait for a favorable moment to get by. The difficulty though was, that Jack had to keep his whole attention fixed on the water, to avoid banging into rocks. The moment he diverted it, he was sure to be rudely admonished by a bump, followed by Tom's cautioning, "Steady there, or you'll have a hole in her." Jack felt that he would have to wait until they reached a smoother place before he could gain the lead.

It was slow work fighting against the stubborn current, which often brought them to a standstill before they were able to find a passage past some dangerously protruding boulder. The river-bed was a mass of rocks both big and little, up one side of which, and down the other, the water rushed, surging and foaming. At last, however, they came to an end of this rapid, and Max's canoe shot stanchly forward into a clear stretch, closely followed by its rival. Jack said to himself, that now was the time to settle the matter. He need no longer worry about rocks ahead.

The water was unruffled, and the bottom was of firm shingle. He threw all his weight into every shove with his pole; and, perceiving that the opponents were making good headway, he turned his head, and said, —

"Now's the chance to hit her up a little, Tom."

So resolute was the spurt that followed, that Joe, who sat facing down river, and could keep his eye on Jack, evidently cautioned his crew to redouble their efforts. Jack realized with pride that he was gaining ground, and began to consider making a final rush. What he tried to do was to creep in between the others and the shore, and crowd them out. But they were quick to perceive his design, and hugged the bank tenaciously.

"No you don't," shouted Hasy with a grin. "Do you take us for countrymen?"

Jack made no reply to this fling. He merely altered the direction of his canoe, so that now it threatened to lap the enemy on the off side, and shoved vigorously.

"Let her go, Gallagher!" cried Joe, who,

though educated abroad, was rapidly learning the vernacular; and Max and Hasy, who had not been making so serious exertions as their rivals, were able to respond nobly to this urgent appeal. For some minutes the canoes maintained the same position, dashing on at a famous pace. Both crews were on the right-hand bank looking up river, and were poling on the left side of the canoes. This last-mentioned circumstance obliged Jack to avoid fouling the poles of his adversaries with his bow, in seeking to pass, as it would have impeded him no less than them. But when, in attempting a final rush, he diverged sufficiently for this purpose, he perceived that he was getting into deeper water. Undismayed, however, he leaned upon his pole with such vim that he could feel it bend, and brought himself abreast of Haseltine, who was in the stern.

"'Now, gallant Saxon, hold thine own!'" he hissed in the ear of his opponent, indulging in a quotation which he knew was familiar to Haseltine.

Not only Hasy but Max heard the warning, who, looking behind him, realized the peril they were in, and suddenly turned the head of the canoe outward so as to force the other farther from the shore.

Struggling madly for the lead, and conse· quently blind as to his course, Jack found himself in deep water, which paralyzed his endeavors. He lunged wildly, seeking still to hold the bottom. These unsteadying motions on his part served to divert his canoe still further, and in another moment he and Tom were beyond the depth of their poles and in the middle of the stream.

"Look out, or you'll have her over," cried Tom, as Jack in his frantic efforts to regain a hold thrust down to right and left.

"Good-by, sweet-heart, good-by," shouted little Joe in delight, kissing his hand as his canoe, turned toward the shore again, darted on.

Poor Jack, boiling with wrath, was quick to appreciate how ludicrous he must appear, vainly pawing the water with his pole, and being carried down stream instead of advancing. The laughter of his rivals, who were all grinning at his plight, was bitter as wormwood.

"Can't you stop her?" he said fiercely to Tom, as the head of the canoe swung across the stream, exposing a broadside to the current. Tom made an ineffectual dab with his pole, realizing the fruitlessness of any such attempts.

"That's no use," shouted Jack. "I'll show you." He plunged his pole eagerly, until only the tip protruded above water. "I've got bottom!" So he had for a moment; but though he held on like a vise, and knelt down so as to bring his arm as near the water as possible, the swift current carried the canoe down in spite of it so as to change the angle of the pole.

"You'll have her over! You'll have her over!" shouted the other two.

This prophecy would immediately have been fulfilled, had not Jack, perceiving that the water was pouring in as a consequence of his leaning over the edge of the canoe, let go the pole to avoid capsizing. He ground his teeth, and seized the paddle beside him as he should have done at first. In this he was imitated by Tom, and a few sweeps enabled them to recover the floating pole and escape from the deep pool.

The boys looked at one another sheepishly. "They've got the laugh on us, that's sure," said Tom.

"Let them laugh; we're not at the Big Salmon Hole yet," was Jack's answer. He could see the victors just disappearing around a bend in the river, after having waited to make sure that no serious mishap had overtaken their victims. Somehow, the only one he felt vindictive against was Max. Not merely because Max had been the immediate cause of his discomfiture, but from a general sense of his own superiority, as Jack would have called it, but which if analyzed was beginning to be closely akin to jealousy. He had made up his mind from the start that Max was beneath notice as a competitor for the rifle, and had dismissed him from his calculations; and yet every day since he had been forced to acknowledge secretly that "the softy" was not quite so despicable as he had at first supposed. It is not agreeable to have to change one's settled convictions, especially when it involves admitting that one assumed to be of no account may possibly become a rival.

"That was a mean trick, I call it," he said, as they resumed their course.

"What?" asked Dubsy.

"Shoving us out into deep water like that. It was just worthy of a tenderfoot."

"That's so," said Dubsy.

"I shouldn't like to have him win the rifle, should you?" Tom remarked after a pause.

"Max?" asked Dubsy.

"Yes."

"Pooh! He hasn't any show. What makes you think he has?" exclaimed Jack sourly.

"He's not so fresh as he was, for one thing," said Tom.

"He's jolly fresh, though, still. A tenderfoot, that's what I call him."

"He stands being knocked round pretty well," continued Tom reflectively. "Did you ever see his hands? They're all cuts and bruises and bites; but he doesn't talk about them."

"That's not much to brag of. Neither did you complain about your feet when you scorched them yesterday."

"No; but then, I've been used to cuts and

burns all my life. I once nearly killed myself with arsenic stuffing a bird."

"I don't see," said Jack, after poling for a few moments in silence, "how a fellow who only knows about books, and can scarcely tell the difference between a base-ball bat and a rifle, and whose skin is as delicate as a girl's, — yes, and isn't able to distinguish a bear cub from a New-foundland pup, can be a better sportsman than you, Tom, or Hasy or Dubsy."

"No-o," replied Tom doubtfully. "Only you know the Colonel said everything would count.'

"Well, if he means that a fellow has got to be able to repeat poetry and do sewing, I'll give up at once." Jack spoke bitterly, having in mind that a day or two before Colonel Russell had spoken in praise of Max's ability to fasten a button on a pair of trousers.

In spite of this professed contempt, Jack was conscious of brooding and of feeling irritated. Although he chose to style the device by which he had been left behind in the race a trick, he knew that Max had really done nothing unsports-manlike. Indeed, the cleverness of the act increased his humiliation. But one point was clear in his mind, — he would give the tenderfoot plenty of occupation to retain his lead to the end. If Max could prevent him from getting by during the whole day, he could afford to crow. It was a little early to do so yet. Thus reflecting, he bent himself to his work again, sturdily seconded by Tom, while Dubsy endeavored to bail out the water that had got in at the time of their catastrophe. As they came round the bend at which the rival canoe had disappeared from view, they came in sight of it once more, not very far ahead.

"What are they trying to do?" said Dubsy, who was the first to notice that it had come to a stand-still.

"Look at that, now," said Jack. "Max is tuckered out already, and Joe is changing places with him. That fellow has no sand."

"I'll take your place, if you're tired," said Dubsy, addressing Tom, whose partial defence of the tenderfoot prompted him to this solicitous inquiry.

"No, thank you, dearest. I'll let you know when I need your assistance."

"It's what I call pusillanimous," continued Jack with indignation. "He keeps the lead by a fluke, and as soon as we get in sight again, backs out of the race. A fine sportsman your friend is."

"I didn't say he was a sportsman," said Tom, resenting the shaft thus directed at him.

"Well, you needn't get mad about it."

"Mad? It's you who are mad. Come, now, I don't see anything very pusillanimous in Max's letting Joe try his hand for a while, if he's tuckered. You're free to do the same, and none of us are fresh as we were. We've got the day before us, and the best crew is the one that comes in first at the Big Salmon Hole. Here, Dubsy, I'll accept your offer," Tom added, putting down his pole; "you take hold, and I'll keep company with Daisy for a mile or so."

"All right," said Jack disdainfully. To tell the truth, he was secretly conscious that Max was very wise. His own exertions had made him feel, as Tom had well expressed it, not as fresh as he had been, and they had many miles to go. However, he would not have admitted it for a hundred dollars. "Hit her up, Dubsy, and we'll pass them," he added.

They started off in fine style, but before Dubsy had made more than a dozen strokes, he managed by ill luck to wedge the point of his socket in between two rocks. Jack, who did not see this, gave the canoe another shove ahead before warned by his companion's cry that anything was wrong.

"Stop her! stop her! Oh!" cried Dubsy, clinging stanchly to the upright pole, and trying by movements from side to side to free it. Just as he was on the point of abandoning it in order not to be pulled out of the canoe, there was 'an ominous sound and out it came. But, on inspection, the point of the pole proved to be badly cracked just above the rim of·the iron socket.

"Bother!" said Dubsy, exhibiting the result to the others.

"How stupid of you!" said Jack in disgust, realizing that the accident would involve making a new point for the socket before they could go on.

"I couldn't help it, Jack," answered Dubsy deprecatingly.

"It was fearful clumsy."

"That isn't true, Jack," said Dubsy quietly, but in such a tone as to show, that, though submissive, he would not put up with more than a certain amount of abuse. He pulled out his jackknife, and cutting off the crushed point began deliberately to scoop out the wood from the socket.

Jack, after an unintelligible growl, turned the canoe to the bank, where he moodily held her during the ten minutes of delay. Not only was he sore against Max, and beginning to despair of being other than a poor third in the race, but he was conscious from the existing silence of having strained his relations for the moment with Tom and Dubsy by his own ill-nature, and so shut himself off from sympathy. He asked himself why he had been so foolish. But still he could not make up his mind to change his tactics.

"All ready," said Dubsy at length, laconically.

Off they started, and for half an hour, while not a word was spoken, made grand progress. Jack's own determined efforts were ably seconded by the faithful Dubsy, who, in spite of the affront put upon him, was true. They had soon caught sight of their opponents; and, though Max was still resting, it gave Jack some satisfaction to see the gap between the canoes diminish. Moreover, the Colonel and Mr. Holt were not so hopelessly in the van as to preclude the possibility of coming up with them. On they went, fighting valiantly against the frequent rapids, until they were fairly dripping with perspiration and nearly exhausted.

"Ready to swap places with either of you fellows," said Tom, breaking the silence. But there was no response save the hard breathing of the polers.

Another quarter of an hour passed, and they were not more than three hundred yards from the canoe ahead, when it stopped again to let Max reassume his post, and Joe change places with Hasy. The sight of this whetted Jack's somewhat panting energies. He buckled to his work, and in a few moments had materially lessened the lead, so that Joe's taunts again became audible.

"Comment vous portez-vous, messieurs? We'd given you up. Thought you'd drifted down to Gaspé Basin by this time. We'll report you as on the way."

Max set a swinging gate for his brother to
follow, and for some little while Jack and Dubsy
could gain no further advantage. Then a low
branch served them by knocking off Max's cap.
By the time it had been fished out, there was not
more than a length between the canoes. Jack felt
weary in every joint, and was puffing like a gram-
pus; yet he was resolved to make one desperate
effort to pass, if he dropped in the attempt. But
now the question arose, as to how to prevent a
repetition of the tactics that had foiled him before.

Max was carefully hugging the shore, and a
glance at the stream satisfied Jack that it was by
no means shallow farther out. As he looked, an
idea suddenly occurred to him, upon which he
immediately began to act by turning the head of
the canoe away from the bank, much to Dubsy's
astonishment, who cried, " What are you trying
to do, Jack?"

"Cross over to the other side. Then they can't
play that dodge on us again." So saying, Jack
sat down, and seizing his paddle sent the canoe
flying across the current by a few deft strokes,
before his comrades had fully appreciated his

intention. Then, without losing a moment after reaching the opposite bank, he gave the signal to Dubsy, and on they went poling with new vim.

Sagacious as was the scheme, Jack had not taken into account that the two banks of a salmon river are not always equally easy of ascent. The rapid by which he was at once beset teemed on their side with ugly rocks and boiling cascades in miniature, while the other canoe, apparently, was finding an easy passage. But on they struggled, taking in water, bumping the canoe, and now and again nearly toppling over themselves, in spite of every effort to use care, and finally brought her through without losing materially on their rivals. Here there was a long piece of still, straight river, at the end of which Jack perceived the Colonel and Mr. Holt hauling up their canoe. It had been given out that they would eat luncheon near a brook called the North Fork, and this was evidently the place.

"It's our last chance," said Jack. "Hit her up lively now." Dubsy nodded, and responded with a will. But the most generous and ambitious spirit cannot avail beyond a certain point. Dubsy

had been working hard, and he was by no means
Jack's equal in physique. Although he plied his
pole with all his remaining energy, he could not
add much to the pace. Still every little was of
service, especially as Jack himself, bare-armed and
bare-headed, his shirt loosened at the neck and
hanging down, was ramming, with set teeth, his
socket against the river-bed, and bending on it all
his sinewy weight, still not quite exhausted, and
eying now the goal and now his adversary. Less
demonstrative in their style, but straining every
nerve, Max and Joe were pressing on, fully alive
to the necessity of making every stroke tell.' The
canoes fairly leaped through the water. Thanks
to his almost superhuman efforts, Jack had undeniably gained a little, — was still gaining. Looking
across the river, he could appreciate this himself.
The enemy's stern almost shut off the other bank
from his view. He caught sight of Hasy, an
interested spectator of the contest, and could tell
from his face that he regarded the victory of the
Fearing pair as by no means assured.

"Hit her up, Dubsy, once more, and we'll get
there," Jack murmured excitedly, while just then

he heard the encouraging shouts, and perceived the waving hats, of the Colonel and Mr. Holt, who evidently understood what was going on. The halting-place now was not more than two hundred yards away, and he was only abreast of Joe. He must pole faster yet, or he would be beaten. Shutting his eyes, he lunged so energetically that his body was almost doubled up.

"Go in, Max; go in, Jack! Well done! The best crew wins."

Max heard the shouts, and they set his blood on fire. He, too, was tired to the bone and scant of breath. His sight was dim with moisture, and his hands raw with blisters; but he knew that he was still ahead, and that there was little farther to go. To beat Jack would be a triumph as sweet as unexpected. Before the race he would have deemed it impossible. If only he could hold out a moment longer, victory was his. Like Jack he shut his eyes, and made half a dozen stalwart shoves, the last of which sent the canoe past the pole which the Colonel had hastily planted upright at the water's edge as a winning-post. He had won.

Jack, beaten by about a length, crossed the river in grim silence. The Colonel and Mr. Holt, who had been congratulating the victors, now came forward to greet the vanquished with smiles slightly sardonic, inasmuch as they knew that Max had hitherto been rated low by the others as an adversary. However, they were not disposed to increase the bitterness of defeat by jibes.

"A close race," said the Colonel judicially.

Jack bit his lip to keep the tears from coming into his eyes.

"They beat us from the start," he managed to utter. The words cost him exertion, but he was glad when they were spoken.

"We shouldn't have come in first, if you hadn't met with so many accidents," said Max. "You know," he added, addressing the elders, "they got into deep water once, where they couldn't pole, and afterwards something else happened."

"Dubsy broke his point," explained Tom.

Jack looked gratefully at Max. He had not expected such magnanimity from a tenderfoot. "What you did was all fair enough," he blurted.

"I'd have forced you out in the same way, if you'd given us the chance."

"Then we rested by turns," said Max. "That made a great difference."

"Yes, you rested," Jack answered slowly. "Dubsy changed places with Tom, too. I feel pretty well tuckered, though," he added.

This last admission was one that Jack would never have made, but from the desire not to be outdone in generosity.

"And so do I," said Max.

"I think you all have rather a dilapidated air," said Mr. Holt.

"I tell you what, though," said Jack pensively; "I'll race you any other day you say, Max, for an equal distance, — you and I alone, each to pole his own canoe; and I'll give you choice of sides of the river."

"I'm willing to try."

"Speaking of dilapidation," broke in the Colonel, who had been examining the canoes, "seems to me the boats have fared worst of all. You boys have got a half hour's work before you in the way of calking, if you expect to get to the

Salmon Hole to-night with a dry skin." · Where-upon he pointed to the numerous indentations and scars on the bottoms of the canoes.

The truth of this comment was very apparent; and while luncheon was being got ready, those not employed in its preparation procured a supply of gum from the spruce-trees, which they melted at the fire, and rubbed over the most serious-looking seams. All the party found re-freshment in laving their faces and hands in the ice-cold water of the North Fork, the broad musical brook which at this point empties into the main river. Then, after taking off the edges of their appetites by a meal of tea, pilot-bread, and potted tongue, the canoes were launched again.

"Now, no more racing, to begin with," said Mr. Holt.

"I was just going to make the same remark myself," said the Colonel. "You're the color of a Stilton cheese, Max; and you needn't look so cocky, Jack, for you're not a bit better. It'll be all you can do, as it is, to get to camp without spurting."

To tell the truth, this was not an unwelcome order to the boys; for, now that the excitement was over, none of them were feeling inclined to repeat the exertions of the morning. Moreover, they found, as the Colonel had foretold, that they needed all their remaining energy to ascend the river in a very leisurely fashion. Although Jack got away from the North Fork before the rival canoe, and saw fit out of pride not to let one of the others take his place at first, it was not long before he gave up, and plumped down beside Daisy. Indeed, there was a general sigh of relief when House No. 2 appeared in sight. This cabin was considerably smaller than the one below, but large enough to afford shelter to all in case heavy rain or the flies should drive them indoors. In front of it lay a long bubbling stretch of dark water, which was the Big Salmon Hole. To fish it one stood on a projecting curve of the bank which overhung the pool, the conformation of the shore here being higher and more rocky. The mountains seemed nearer than before, and shut them in on every side. The walls inside the little house were decorated with the scores of former anglers, inspiring testimony as to what might be hoped for in the way of fish.

It may well have been that the boys secretly yearned for the assistance of old William and Jimmy to assist them after the hard day's journey; but, nevertheless, they set to work industriously to make tent-poles, collect firewood and hemlock, and perform the various tasks incident to pitching camp. The sun had set and the twilight was deepening into darkness before supper was on the table. The half of a salmon brought from below staved off for another day at least salt-pork fare; and after they had eaten every scrap of it, in addition to some hot canned soup which tasted uncommonly good, all sought and encircled the grand fire which Mr. Holt and Joe had built to neutralize the chill, which, at this higher altitude, is apt to come over the atmosphere of the woods in midsummer. It seemed quite frosty, in fact, so that overcoats felt very comfortable to the overheated boys.

"Well," said Mr. Holt, casting his eyes up at the clear heavens now studded with stars, and sniffing the air odorous with the aroma of the tall pines that towered up on every side, "this is what I call camping out. I don't like the idea of paying a man to do what one really ought to do for himself, in order to be a thorough woodsman. Now there are no masters and no servants."

"No, only masters and boys," said Max with a laugh.

"I don't think the distinction is a very marked one," said the Colonel. "For the matter of that, we're all boys out here in the woods. At least, I claim to be. We'll let the Big Medicine Man speak for himself."

"Pray don't let the distinction be made on my account," said Mr. Holt, "if I am the person referred to. Indeed, I am the most of a boy of any in the party; for the rest of you take life so seriously, — fishing, hunting, and poling as if vital interests depended on the result of your individual powers: whereas I am, so to speak, volatile, — content to cast a little, and smoke a little, and paddle a little, and read a little, and watch the clouds a little, and eat a great deal, — each as the humor seizes me. Consequently, I suppose, the Colonel will claim that I don't enjoy myself."

"It isn't my way of enjoying myself, certainly," exclaimed Colonel Russell, "and — Well, go on. Let's hear what you were going to say."

"I know it isn't; and, of course," continued the master, relighting his pipe, "I" — puff — "don't wish for a moment" — puff — "to say a word against the so-called genuine sportsman" — puff —

"You'd better not," said the Colonel. "Had he, boys?"

"No!" was the unanimous cry, which showed where the sympathies of the audience were for the moment.

"You boys wait until I'm through," said Mr. Holt, "and then you may shout as much as you please. As I was going to say, when interrupted, the Colonel is an admirable character, a thorough-going sportsman in every sense; and as such it behooves him, and I can understand why it should interest him, to pursue indefatigably salmon or bear or whatever the game of the region where he happens to be is, up early, and returning to camp late, regardless of rain, heat, flies, and never idle a moment. That is the programme to be followed by the man or boy who wishes to make a large bag, and be spoken of as a Mighty Hunter (accept this epithet in return for Medicine Man). I am the last person to regard otherwise than with profound admiration the triumphs of such unwearying ardent spirits; and in claiming toleration for the less energetic clan, of which I am in a certain sense representative, let me acknowledge frankly, that the angler who gives up after casting over a pool once or twice in an airy fashion, and passes on to the next one, or hands his rod to his boatman to try with while he reads a novel, must renounce all claim to being looked on as a first-rate fisherman."

"I should think so, forsooth," cried the Colonel. "The only thing to be said in favor of such fair-weather individuals is, that by their failure to comb the pools for fish, and beat the bushes for birds, there is more chance for the persevering kind to kill the game that would have fallen to them had they been diligent."

"Precisely. We acknowledge our degradation; and all we ask is that we be permitted to enjoy ourselves in our own way, and that you sporting swells do not keep telling us forever that we are not enjoying ourselves.   Incredible as it may seem, there are many excellent people who derive more satisfaction from the surroundings of camp-life than from the sport itself.   Men's tastes differ as much in the woods as in the midst of civilization; and, while one is keen in pursuing game, another would scarcely walk a mile to kill a bear or a moose, — might even think it a bore, — and yet delight in the woods all the same."

"Hear him!" said the Colonel disdainfully. "Ye gods and little fishes, think it a bore to kill a moose!   Show me the man."

"The woods are full of them," was the imperturbable answer.   "There is many a busy man whose only escape from the worries of business is to plunge into the forest primeval, where no telegram or letter can find him, and there luxuriate doing nothing; letting fish, if they will, fasten themselves on to his hook, or birds peep into the barrel of his gun, but not taking it much to heart if they fail to do so.   Or, again, there is the clergy-man or quiet scholar, to whom the use of gun or rod is wholly unfamiliar, and to whom paddling or wood-chopping or botanizing furnishes recreation more congenial than tracking bears or following twenty-pound salmon over rapids."

"Ah, yes!" said the Colonel. "But the clergyman or quiet scholar would be all the more of a man for learning how to use a rod or gun, and the business man had better let the fish alone, and not stir up the pools, if he doesn't care whether he kills any or not."

The boys laughed at this sally.

"But supposing they prefer not to follow your advice,—though I dare say it would be well if they did, in many cases,—what I maintain," said Mr. Holt quietly, "is that they who lead this lazy life are as able to appreciate the beauties of Nature quite as much, if not more, than you other fellows who will follow a deer from sunrise to sunset. You genuine sportsmen are cranks in a certain way. You believe that no one can enjoy himself except by imitating you. There, put that in your pipe and smoke it. Mine has gone out from too much talking."

"A crank, eh! Do you hear that, my young Nimrods? This ease-loving master of yours calls us cranks. Well, then, we are cranks—enthusiasts — whatever you choose; but, in that case, so were Isaac Walton and Humphry Davy. Do you believe that either of them would have admitted for a moment that the forest and the stream and the birds and the hues of morning and evening are as intelligible to one who fishes merely to kill time, and knows nothing of tackle and flies, as to an ardent follower of the sport they loved so well ? "

" Very likely not," — puff, — " but that doesn't alter my opinion."

" Bah ! I disown you," said the Colonel. " Boys, henceforth you have to choose between your master and me. Under which king, Bezonian ? "

" Hurrah for Colonel Russell," cried Jack.

" That's so," said Dubsy, and a cheer that seemed general followed.

" I'm sure," said Hasy, who had been lost in thought, " that when I'm playing a base-ball match I always enjoy a fine day or a beautiful sky more than at other times."

Every one laughed loudly at this pertinent testimony to the point of the discussion, and the Colonel exclaimed with rapture, "Of course you do, Hasy."

"I seem to be in a decided minority," said Mr. Holt, when the mirth had subsided. "But I'm not at all disconcerted thereby. You boys are quite right to model yourselves on the Colonel. His theory is more inspiriting than mine. But I shall, in spite of his and your displeasure, reserve the right as Medicine Man to enjoy my own opinion as to the capabilities for enjoyment which those of my less persevering disposition possess. Moreover, I will take my revenge upon you all at the moment, by breathing the mystic word — bed-time."

In spite of some little outcry, none were averse to being reminded that the day had been exhausting, and not many minutes after the boys had separated to their quarters. The cabin was unoccupied, as there seemed to be a general opinion that the tents were less stuffy. Mr. Holt shared one with the Colonel, who as soon as they were out of hearing remarked, —

"What should you think of our letting two of the boys go up to the Narrows, and camp by themselves for a few days?"

"Alone?"

"Yes," said the Colonel. "It seems to me that it might be a good experience for them, and that they would scarcely run a greater risk by themselves than if with us. To tell the truth," he added, "there is not enough fishing below here to keep us all busy, and the pools above are sure to be full of salmon. There's a rough log cabin a little way below the falls, in which they could live, as, owing to the low condition of the river, they couldn't get a canoe up even as far as the Indian Falls: so they wouldn't want to carry a tent or any other luggage not absolutely necessary. There's an old canoe of mine up there that would answer their purpose for fishing. I'll go up with them, — it's only four miles, but Gaspé miles with windfalls every hundred yards, — and get them established. How does it strike you?"

"I see no objection," answered the master. "Indeed, it strikes me as altogether a sensible plan. Have you any two of the boys especially in mind?"

The Colonel shook his head.

"Then I think it would be a good idea if we let Jack and Max be the two," said Mr. Holt. "You may not have noticed that there is a quiet rivalry between them, which I think is having a good effect on both. Jack began, in common with the others, by looking down on Max, and he is, I judge, still trying to persuade himself that he is justified in doing so; but one or two such experiences as he had this morning will open his eyes, if they are not open already, to the fact that he has no nonentity to deal with."

"Max is improving, certainly," said the Colonel. "I was, as you know, rather tempted to share Jack's opinion of him at the start; but he is not lacking in grit, I will do him the justice to say, however much in need of experience he may be. He handled the gun yesterday as if he didn't know the butt from the muzzle, and yet he tramped right along for six hours without uttering a word of complaint."

"Jack is likely to learn from him that one may be scholarly and book-loving in his tastes without being a 'softy' or a weakling," continued Mr. Holt. "On the other hand, he will derive, from competition with Jack, a stimulus to become more manly, and needed training for his muscles. If it seems best to you, we will let them be companions at the Narrows; and, as they are the biggest two of the party, we can give that as our reason for the selection, in case of general competition for the privilege."

The plan thus decided on was laid before the boys next morning, and met with general approval, inasmuch as the chances for fish for those remaining at the Big Salmon Hole would be improved by the departure of two such keen anglers as Jack and Max. Jack himself, while delighted at the opportunity offered, did not regard with enthusiasm the choice of his associate. Forgetting or regardless of the episode of the previous day, he made the reflection that Max, to keep pace with him, would have to alter his ladylike ways, and show more gumption. If not, he would have to shift for himself. Jack had no idea of playing nurse, and endeavored to convey an impression to this effect by a few hints which he dropped when the elders were out of hearing.

The two boys were not to start until the following day, in order that they might explore the present surroundings. The Colonel went out before breakfast, and, standing on the projecting ledge referred to, landed in quick succession three fine salmon, which relieved all present anxiety on the score of fresh food.

"There was a time, boys," said Mr. Holt, as they settled down fifteen minutes later to some slices cut from one of the shining beauties, "when salmon were so plentiful in the State of Maine,—which was then a part of Massachusetts,—that factory apprentices used to stipulate in their contracts that they should not be obliged to eat it more than a certain number of days in the week."

"Here it is Hobson's choice," said the Colonel. "But if none of you ever have to eat anything worse than salmon, you may count yourself lucky. I've sucked buffalo skin on the plains, and been grateful for roast horse."

After the meal was over, the Colonel resigned his post to Mr. Holt, and piloted all the boys but Dubsy and Joe, detained by camp duties, down to the pools below,—the Still Pool, the Dog Pool, and Maitland's, out of which respectively two, four. and three salmon were taken by him, Tom, and Hasy, the allotted anglers of the day. The sport was excellent. The fish not having been disturbed before this season were in rising humor, and snapped at whatever fly one chose to cast, be it Jock Scott, Cock Robin, Prince of Orange, Black Dose, Silver Doctor, or Fairy.

All the boys were by this time excellent anglers, and Hasy had the good fortune to land at Maitland's a thirty-five and a half pounder, the largest fish yet taken, in sixteen minutes, a vivid contrast to Jack's five hours' experience. But, as the Colonel remarked at the time, the largest salmon in a river are apt to be more logy than those five or ten pounds lighter. Indeed, Hasy confided to Jack disappointment that the monster had not pulled more.

The description of the capture of one salmon is to a certain extent that of all, but to the angler there is variety in every fish encountered. He who starts after breakfast, and returns at nightfall with two or three, has had a successful day; and there are few sensations more agreeable than the consciousness that the heap of alder-bushes at one's feet in the canoe conceals a noble twenty pounder landed after a gallant struggle for life and liberty. In a good year, there are days when one may bag five, six, seven, eight, or nine, and lose two or three more, and even then be in no danger of breaking the record of a single twelve hours' sport; but this is exceptional good fortune. As the Colonel observed on returning to camp this evening, the aggregate for the day of fourteen fish to four rods — Mr. Holt had killed three besides the others enumerated — was a record of which any party had a right to be proud.

Indeed, it is to be said, that he who kills one fine salmon in a day has no just cause to murmur; he is a happy being. Let him recall the number of blank days he has experienced. And those blank days are very blank, — blankety, blankety, blank, to quote our friend Jack's expression regarding one of them. Patience at such times is a virtue of the noblest order, as indeed it ought always to be regarded. And a first-rate sportsman is always patient.

CHAPTER VII.

THE RIVALS.

THE path to the Narrows led through thick woods, though it could be called a path only by courtesy. Large trunks had fallen across it, grass and moss had grown over it, and the blaizes on the trees had become obscure. It was made use of only by a few anglers in summer, and the Gaspé men who in winter-time went up to the hills to shoot caribou. The Colonel tramping first with axe in hand did some strenuous clearing of the underbrush, and knocked out splinters in an occasional pine or birch along the way, so that Nature might not be able to boast of having oblit-erated every trace of civilization. Behind him stalked Jack and Max, proud of their coming liberty; and all three were laden with the indis-pensable paraphernalia for a week's outing, — blankets, a kettle, a gun, a gaff, the rods, a rubber bag containing a change of clothing for each boy, and another into which had been stuffed sundry stores and an accumulation of necessary odds and ends (such as matches, twine, soap, towels; a knife, fork, and spoon apiece; some tin plates and two tin cups, and a lantern). The kit had been made as small as possible; otherwise, the young sportsmen would have fallen by the way under the press of their burdens. But, as it was, they were able to march along with tolerable comfort.

Though the distance was said to be but four miles, they were certainly the genuine Gaspé miles the Colonel had foretold them to be, equal, at least as far as one's impressions were concerned, to six of the ordinary sort. Jumping over or climbing round windfalls, when one is laden like a mule, is not the most exhilarating form of exercise. But, while Jack had no high opinion of it as sport, he took good care not to let Max suspect that he felt in any way hampered by what he was carrying. He whistled, and now and then ran a few yards, to show how indifferent he was to his load. In attempting, however, to clear a fallen tree at a bound, instead of going round it, he

came so near pitching headlong, that he was reminded of his recent fiasco, and resolved to confine
within less dangerous limits his inclination for
display.

"How do you like it as far as you've got?" he
inquired patronizingly of his companion, down
whose face the perspiration was streaming as a not
unnatural result of wearing a knapsack across his
back, and carrying one of the rubber bags swung
over one of his shoulders, and the bundle of rods
in the other hand.

"Rather warm work, isn't it?"

"Not especially.   I feel first-rate.   Want me to
take those rods for you?"

Max smiled and shook his head.   Though he
appeared grateful, he would have been very slow
to avail himself of the offer.

The path was pretty straight in spite of its
difficulties, whereas the river wound in and out,
so that they rarely were within sight of it; but
they could from time to time hear the murmur of
the rapids, which presently became so loud that
the Colonel exclaimed, —

"We'll have a look at the Indian Falls, boys."

Whereupon he dropped the various articles which he was carrying, and led the way at right angles from their course in the direction of the river. The boys, having imitated his example, followed, and, after struggling through the intricacies of the forest for a few moments, they reached the bank. In front was an expanse of seething foam, the first-fruits of the cascade, which but just above fell in a swift tawny deluge some eight feet high. Farther up, as far as they could see, the river came tearing down, billowy and churning.

"How should you like to run that, Jack?" asked the Colonel.

"In a canoe? Golly! I should think it would smash her all to pieces."

"The chances would be decidedly that way," was the dry answer.

For a few moments they all watched the waterfall without speaking. There was a fascination in the smooth way in which the galloping flood slipped over the verge and dropped in a shimmering wall below.

"I should think it would get tired," said Max.

"It does occasionally," said their guide. "That is to say, the water becomes low in the river, and the rocks begin to show themselves; and, though the fall always exists, it loses in force and picturesqueness.

"Did any one ever run it in a canoe?" asked Jack, who had been brooding over the earlier dialogue.

"I have never seen any one attempt it. The men in former years have been fond of boasting of their ability to do so; but, when it came to the point, I have noticed that they were apt to say the water was either too low or too high."

"But how does one manage to come down, then?" asked Max.

"Carry round it," answered Jack with an air of superiority.

"Yes," said the Colonel. "The canoes used to stop a little piece above here, and the men carried them on their shoulders the necessary distance. But, owing to the inconvenience of this, a canoe has for the last few years been kept at the Narrows, so that no one often troubles the falls nowadays."

After a few minutes of further inspection, the onward march was resumed, not to be interrupted again until they reached the log cabin. This proved to be an unsealed and rather gaping-looking affair, exposed, on account of crevices between the logs, to the inroads of the man or beast that might from curiosity or desire for shelter seek an entrance. In fact, as the Colonel, after unfastening the padlock, let in the light, there was a clattering along the floor, and a creature the size of a small dog was descried in a corner of the single apartment. On the approach of the visitors, it contracted itself into a round ball, and appeared to be bristling all over with quills.

"A hedgehog," said the Colonel. "Lucky for Bingo that he is absent, or he would stand a chance of carrying off some arrows in his snout. These fellows are very clever at eating their way into houses in the woods," he added, calling the attention of the boys to a hole that had been gnawed in the flooring.

By means of prodding with the butt of the gaff, the prickly beast was banished from the cabin without injury either to it or its ejectors: and after tidying the place a little, and bestowing their belongings, Jack and Max put their rods together, and set off with the Colonel to learn the positions of the pools. The canoe, a birch-bark one, was found in the loft, and in it a pair of paddles. Two poles were soon manufactured, and shod with sockets. As the canoes they had been using hitherto were of wood, the boys found themselves for the first few minutes a little at sea, but they soon got accustomed to the somewhat different action of the new skiff. After leaving the house, the river began to grow narrower and narrower, running swiftly between bold, sheer precipices on either side, now thickly wooded and now bare, but skirted usually at the base by a narrow beach of sand, until at last the banks were not more than thirty feet apart. At this point, there was a roaring rapid, at the head of which the walls opened out into a broad, expansive pool, the sanctuary of hundreds of salmon, so said the Colonel. It was a beautiful spot; its surface a dark, placid mirror, flecked here and there with patches of snowy foam which had sailed down from the fall a little way above.

"Whoever hooks a fish in that pool has to kill him there," said the Colonel. "If he gets into the rapid, he bids you good-by."

This was not difficult of belief, especially as the boys had just had all they could do to force the canoe through the torrent in question. After a few moments' delay, keeping close to the shore so as not to disturb the fish, they passed on through a chain of pools — one of them of unusual length — to the graceful fall half a mile above, under which the salmon were accustomed to congregate in large numbers prior to taking the daring leap that gave them access to still more distant spawning beds. As a waterfall, the cascade was not very imposing, — much less so, the Colonel said, than those in many other salmon rivers; but the volume of water was high and broad enough to cause Jack and Max to wonder how the finny aspirants could manage to ascend it. They crept up to within a few yards of the cataract, where they held the canoe steady with their paddles, so close to it that they could feel the light spatter of the spray. As, spell-bound, they were watching the translucent down-pour, a salmon suddenly jumped out of water just ahead, quivered for a moment in mid-air, and fell back again into its native element with a splash.

"That fellow was taking a look to see how high it was," said the Colonel.

Soon after they had the good fortune to witness a successful attempt on the part of another fish, which, keeping close to the wall of rock, using a ledge here and a ledge there as a breathing-place, and obtaining impetus by standing on its tail, swam up the cataract. Max, as the triumphant climber darted forward out of sight, inquired, —

"What is there beyond, — farther up river?"

"Very much the same sort of thing you have seen below, for twenty miles or so, and then the lake."

"Could we go up?" asked Jack.

"There would be no difficulty after you had carried the canoe round this fall, but the trip would scarcely pay you. I went up some years ago, and found the fishing only tolerable, and the scenery not especially fine. The salmon are more scattered and congregate less in pools."

"But wouldn't there be a better chance of seeing big game?" asked Jack.

"Not a bit. Max's old adversary is just as likely to learn of your being up here alone as if you were to go up farther. You'd better be on your guard, by the way; for, if she should happen to get wind of it, she might take it into her head to organize a prowling party to make reprisal for the loss of her cubs."

"I wish she would," said Jack, and Max nodded approval of this bold sentiment.

Before returning to the Big Salmon Hole, the Colonel cast a fly over the long pool, and in less than an hour had landed two large fish, and lost a third. Then the boys prepared him a lunch, after which he bade them good-by for a fortnight, as he said.

Two persons alone in the woods cannot escape each other's society. Fishing side by side, sitting together by the same fire at night, and sharing the same tent, with no one else to speak to, opens

one's eyes wonderfully, alike to the blemishes and
the fine points in a companion's character. Jack,
as we know, had come away with an indeterminate
idea of setting a very lively pace for Max to follow,
so as to put him in the shade or tire him out
by his own activity and energy. He began accordingly to devote himself with the utmost assiduity
to his rod, rising early, and ceasing to fish only
when lack of daylight rendered further casting
useless. Moreover, he cut down trees and cooked
with equal enthusiasm, seeming to scorn fatigue,
and to wish to take upon his shoulders all the
work. In the evening he led the conversation to
the various sports of which his companion was
ignorant, hinting at his own proficiency therein,
and singing the praises of rowing and base-ball,
and the manly art of self-defence, in a way adapted,
as he thought, to make Max experience shame and
envy, and ask himself, "Am I not a flub-dub?"
This was an expression Jack had applied to him,
not openly, as he had no excuse for a row, but
covertly in his own thoughts.

Meantime Max disappointed him by not appearing in the least exhausted by the daily routine of

pleasure and duty, and in nowise inclined to faint by the wayside, or to allow himself to be out-stripped either in fishing or in work. The flub-dub, so called, certainly made no complaints, but was perfectly willing to get up in the morning as soon as it was light, insisted on taking part in collecting fire-wood and preparing breakfast, and gave him no opportunity to make a bigger score on the river by idling or ceasing to fish before he did; and with it all was thoroughly good natured, listening to the accounts of rowing and base-ball exploits with friendly interest, and yet without seeming disheartened thereby. Jack had hardly bargained for this.

As they had but one canoe, and as neither was skillful enough as yet to gaff his own fish while holding the rod, as they had seen the Colonel do, the boys kept near each other while fishing; the one casting from the beach where it was possible, while the other cast from the canoe. The salmon rose wonderfully. On the day after the Colonel's departure they took four apiece, and on the next the fishing was fairly grand. Jack landed seven, and Max lost his seventh from its wriggling off the gaff. They had agreed that when a fish was ready for gaffing, the one whose fish it was should pass his rod to his companion, and perform himself the delicate operation of gaffing. So it was none of Jack's fault that this fish was lost; and, as it would have tied his score, Jack could not help feeling a little secret satisfaction. But two days later the salmon was found floating dead in an eddy, and it seemed to him as though fate were opposed to his shaking off Max.

After the third day the fish rose less keenly, and the boys were not sorry on the afternoon of the fifth to see the sun go down behind a bank of clouds. Rain followed before morning, a drenching drizzle at first, which increased by breakfast time into heavy showers. Jack persisted in fishing, to which Max made no demur beyond remarking that the Colonel had told them that salmon rarely would take the fly during a storm.

"You can never be sure until you try," said Jack laconically.

Accordingly they tried for three hours, attired in rubber coats and boots, without getting a rise.

Moist and clammy, for it was hot, they returned to the log cabin. Here the time went slowly, especially for Jack. Max had his volume of poetry with him, from which he offered to read aloud; but our hero would none of it. After sunset the rain ceased, and later on the moon broke through the clouds. As it had not been possible to make a fire, they had lived on cold rations during the day, and now Jack had curled himself in his ulster and laid down. Max wandered down to the water's edge. The night was rapidly becoming fine. A favorable breeze had banished the scud, and was driving the cloud-bank, through which the moon had pierced, down behind the tree-tops. The river, showing already the effects of the severe rain, was running fiercely, and reflected the alternate light and shade of the heavens.

"Jack!" called Max, inspired to share the spectacle.

"What?" came the drowsy answer.

"You ought to see the sky. It's very fine."

There was no response. Evidently the subject did not appeal to him within doors, or he was not disposed to humor his comrade's poetical proclivities. A few moments later Max called again, but this time his tone expressed importunity and mystery combined.

"Jack, come here quick."

The drowsy sportsman jumped to his feet straightway, and ran out into the night; but seeing Max standing at the water's edge, seemingly imperturbed, he changed his gait to a saunter, and said a little querulously, —

"Well, here I am."

"Come quick," repeated Max, in a low tone.

Jack, again impressed, hastened his footsteps.

"Do you see anything?" Max asked, pointing across the river a little up stream. "I have lost it now," he added, "but I could almost swear I saw a canoe close to the opposite bank."

"A canoe! Whose canoe?"

"I don't know. It crossed one of those bright streaks, and I saw it as plainly as could be. Then it passed beyond, and I have not seen it again. There was one man poling."

"Going up stream?"

"Yes."

Jack was shading his eyes with one hand, and staring fixedly. Some thin clouds had partially obscured the moon, so that the light on the river was fitful and less effulgent.

"I can't see anything," he said decidedly.

"Very possibly it was imagination," said Max. "Though I saw the canoe for a moment with perfect distinctness," he added, evidently reluctant to admit that he had been deceived. "I don't suppose there are such things as phantom barks, do you?"

"Pshaw! no," answered Jack. "You've been reading a lot of that silly stuff, which has made you fancy you saw something, I guess."

"Poetry, do you mean?" asked Max, surprised.

"Yes."

In spite of his disdainful disclaimer of a disbelief in the supernatural, Jack seemed reflective, and after gazing up river for a few minutes longer inquired,—

"What did the canoe look like?"

"Like any other canoe."

"It's queer, certainly, if you weren't dreaming."

"I was just as much awake as you are now,

Jack. It may have been an hallucination, of course. But it's what I call weird."

As there was no way of solving the mystery, bed seemed the best place. In the morning they found the fish quite eager to rise, owing doubtless to the discoloration of the water by the rain. The river was manifestly swollen, and had risen at least a foot during the night. After killing four salmon, and losing one or two others, they drew the canoe ashore at the Narrows pool, and prepared lunch. Just as they had finished, Max, who was looking across the river, suddenly whispered, —

"Look, Jack."

"It's a bear," was the awe-struck, delighted answer.

Sure enough, on the opposite bank, busily engaged in gnawing the end of a log, was a splendid brown specimen of the ursine tribe. The boys were in the shade, and not directly exposed to the creature's view; but they could not reach their canoe, in which lay the gun, without running the risk of attracting its attention.

"We must get a shot at him," said Jack, and

he began to creep on all fours down the bank. By stealthy movements, he managed to reach the shore without disturbing the bear, and had reached out his hand for the gun, when there came a sudden quawk, quawk, quawk, and a shell-drake started up from the sedge a few feet beyond, and stretching out its long neck went screeching down the river, so startling Jack that he jumped, and joggled one of the poles which lay across a thwart. Bruin heard the clatter, and looking up spied Jack. Rising, he pawed the air for a moment, but dropped to earth and disappeared in the thicket, before Jack, who had grabbed the gun, could draw a bead on him.

"Come on," cried Jack, in a guttural whisper, and immediately leaped into the canoe, and seized a paddle.

Max was at his side in an instant, and they glided swiftly across the pool.

"We'd better pull her up high and dry, and tip her over. No telling when we may get back," said Jack feverishly, as they landed. He had usurped the leadership, and he had also seized

the rifle, which was in their joint custody. If
it passed through his mind that this was ungen-
erous, he did not choose to think of it. "Come
on," he reiterated, after they had disposed of the
canoe, and he plunged into the underbrush.

But there was nothing to be seen. The woods
were still. At first they were dismayed; then,
remembering their former experience, they set to
work to examine the ground, which, soft after the
storm, would be likely to reveal tracks. These
were found after a search of a few minutes,
and followed enthusiastically. Carried away by
excitement, they hurried through the forest, not
knowing whither, and careless as to how they
should get back. So long as the traces of the
hunted animal could be discerned on moss or
leaves, the pursuers thought of nothing else.
Their energies were devoted to preserving the
trail, and finding it again when lost. For a
moment it did occur to Max that they might be
losing themselves, and he gave vent to the
unavailing regret, —

"I wish we had an axe with which to blaize
some of these trees."

"If only we find the bear," answered Jack, "I don't care what happens."

"Neither do I."

On they trudged, deep into thickets, up wooded knolls and down into morasses, across patches of open country rough with charred stumps, and again into almost gloomy pine groves where tall and spreading trees did their best to shut out the blue sky, and fungus growths ran riot at their feet. Jack still led the way, and Max followed. Suddenly our hero stopped short, and exclaimed in the tone of one aghast, —

"Thunder! Have you any cartridges?"

Max turned pale. "No," he faltered.

"That's a pretty mess to be in, isn't it? Idiot that I am, I left them in the canoe."

"But she's loaded," said Max.

"Yes, we can have one shot, anyway. Feel in your pockets."

Each did so, but the search was fruitless. The charge in the gun was their only-ammunition. Max looked at his watch. It was half-past three. They had been tramping more than two hours.

On they went, until the slanting rays and the

increasing somberness of the shade warned them that darkness was not far off. But what manly boy would the prospect of a night in the woods without food or shelter appall, if such a prize as Bruin could be secured thereby? Yet where was Bruin? Even his tracks were found and lost and found again; and still no glimpse of his brown hide was caught, no growl rewarded the alert ears of his untiring pursuers. From time to time Jack shifted the rifle from one shoulder to the other, but this was their only tribute to fatigue.

Where could Bruin be?

They reached at last a bosky bourn, as a poet would say, a dell deeply shaded, out of which a quiet brook bubbled, scarcely perceptible at times, so overgrown was it with green things, but deep enough to dampen the ardor of one who trod therein disdainfully. The trickling water was perceived by Jack just in time to enable him to pause upon the margin. Thirst fully as much as discretion bade him do so. He fell upon his knees and lapped the cool rill, beast fashion, boy fashion, and dipped his perspiring brow twice and thrice. Max did the same. Then, as their gaze diverged in search of the precious trail, it was seen that Bruin had paused likewise to drink, and that his claws had left their imprint in such a fashion as to show that he had dallied and dawdled.

"He may be round here," said Jack; and while speaking his face was illumined by hope.

The tracks were on both banks of the spring. They ran along it in one direction upon the hither side, ran back again still farther in the opposite way, crossed it and kept close to the edge for two hundred yards, until opposite the point from which they had originally started. Here Bruin had pawed up the ground over a small area, from mere sportiveness apparently, and incident to wallowing to some extent in the cool water. Then the footprints led off obliquely through the wood again.

"He has rested, so we must have gained on him," said Max.

As he uttered the words, a dull tearing sound was audible, which seemed to proceed from behind a large decayed tree-trunk a short distance ahead. The boys listened intently, and immediately the noise was repeated, resembling that produced by rudely rending rotten wood.

"It's him," said Jack, no less oblivious of grammar than the monks who detected the Jackdaw of Rheims. "You stay here," he continued, "and I'll reconnoiter."

So saying, he stalked circuitously, on his belly or on tiptoe, from tree to tree, until he reached a point which commanded a view of the reverse of the decayed trunk. It was decayed, certainly,—rather, it was hollow,—and standing upright, with teeth buried in the punk-like timber near the top, was the big bear. Bruin's head reached just about on a level with the height of the broken tree, so that he was concealed from any one standing on the other side. At his feet was a mangled piece of carcass, which looked like the remains of a deer. On this he had evidently been lately feeding. What was he doing? Investigating to discover suitable sleeping quarters?

Jack was in no state of mind for conjecture. He squatted down behind his own tree, and beckoned vigorously to Max, who succeeded in joining him without giving notice of their presence to the enemy. The next move required serious consideration. Their single shot spent in vain, what could they do? From where they were, a good marksman ought not to miss; but, on the other hand, could either of them be called a good marksman? Jack did not believe Max to be, and at heart he felt grave doubts as to his own ability. But something must be done. To have come such a distance, and not to make an attempt to slay so grand a prize, was out of the question. Jack nervously fingered the rifle, and went so far as to cock it.

"Are you sure you can hit him from here," Max asked.

"I'm not certain exactly which is a mortal spot," answered Jack evasively.

The bear was still busy with its investigations. But just after Jack's remark it stopped and sniffed apprehensively.

"I guess he smells us."

"He's a big fellow, isn't he? He could chew us into mince-meat if he got hold of us," said Max.

"I don't mean to let him get hold of us. See here," Jack continued resolutely, "I'm going to try to creep up on him, and get close enough to fire before he sees me. I don't dare to risk it from here."

Thereupon he stepped cautiously from behind the tree, and began to advance. The distance from him to the bear was about eighty yards, and there was nothing but open space between them. The ground, however, was so mossy, that by treading lightly footfalls need not be audible. With his rifle cocked and grasped before him, ready to aim at once if the beast should turn, Jack traversed successfully half the space, and then stood still. To come to very close quarters with such a monster would be scarcely prudent, if he could be sure of doing equal execution farther off. Even Jack's stout spirit recognized this. With the idea of testing how sure an aim he could get at the present distance, he dropped upon one knee.

But just then Bruin began to move, and to let himself drop upon all fours by slipping down the trunk; not apparently because suspicious, — for after his sniffing fit he had placidly resumed his labors, — but doubtless for the reason that he had now finished them.

Jack felt himself quivering all over. He took rigid aim at the shaggy bulk; but the backing and turning process which Bruin was indulging in was confusing, and convinced him that this was no moment for one with but a single rifle-ball at his disposal to fire. Round wheeled the bear, unconscious of danger, and presenting for a moment a tempting flank. But, though Jack's finger half contracted on the trigger, he could not satisfy himself that he had just the right aim before it was. too late. Then he beheld facing him two yellow eyes and a huge snout, and a mouth which afforded a flashing glimpse of white, savage teeth, as the brute, apprised of peril, opened it to express its feelings in a blood-curdling growl. If unwise to fire before, it was surely so now, with his enemy standing head on in such a way that an experienced marksman might well fail to hit a vital spot. In the awful moment of suspense that followed the growl, during which each surveyed the other and made no movement, he could not help wishing that he had fired when the chance had been given him to get a shot at the creature's broad side. It seemed an eternity to Jack. The yellow eyes, dilating as they gazed, were fixed upon him with ominous scrutiny, which he, remembering that animals are said to quail before a resolute human stare, endeavored to return. There came another growl, louder and more menacing than the first, and Bruin rose upon his hind legs with the evident design of advancing to seize the rash intruder on his privacy. Jack felt that the time for action on his part had come. Still crouching, with one knee on the ground, he put the rifle to his shoulder, took aim at the heart, and, as the bear danced angrily forward, pulled the trigger. He heard what seem to him half a scream and half a roar. He sprang to his feet, confused a little by the report and smoke. Was Bruin dead, he asked himself, or had he missed? The next moment he was conscious of two yellow eyes become balls of fire, and that a hairy mass was sweeping down upon him. He sprang back, putting out instinctively his gun before him as a barrier between him and destruction. It was torn from his grasp by terrible violence, at the same moment that two rows of white, savage teeth gleamed cheek by jowl with him. Seeking to escape, Jack threw himself away from them with all his power; and as he did so his heels caught in a creeping vine, and he fell heavily backwards. "Max!" he screamed, in the agony of despair; and at the moment thoughts of home and his mother and all the panorama of his past life rose before him. Even in that brief spell he had time to reflect that if he were spared he would try to become a better fellow.

There was no need of that cry to warn Max of his comrade's frightful peril. Breathless and trembling with excitement, he had beheld from his post behind the tree, without stirring, the first scenes in the drama which led to the bear's perception of his enemy. Instinctively, as he saw Bruin rise from the earth in growling majesty, he had clutched and unsheathed his knife, and stepped forward. Why did not Jack fire? Then had come the flash, cutting short his quivering mood, followed by a shriek of pain. Peering forward in the full belief—such was his confidence in Jack's powers—that the bear had fallen, he was suddenly confronted by a sight that thrilled him with horror. The monster, instead of lying prostrate on the ground, stood erect and rampant, and was advancing, apparently uninjured, in full fury upon his adversary.

Max's impulse was to fly for self-preservation; but, though he drew back, the fascination of horror rooted his feet. Spell-bound, as it were, he saw the maddened beast snatch at, and beat down, the interposed rifle, and Jack himself fall over backwards in a futile effort to escape, uttering his name in an agonized cry. There was no time for indecision. In another instant the infuriated animal would have his teeth in its vanquished enemy's throat. With a swift glance at the knife in his hand, the blade of which, thanks to the supervision of the Colonel, was no apology for a weapon, but a long sharp piece of steel, Max darted forward with uplifted arm, and struck the bear with all his might and main before the creature, too devoted to its desire for vengeance to regard a new antagonist, could ward off the blow aimed at its exposed left breast. Such was his impetus, that, as the blade buried itself, he was brought into close contact with the bear's body, then fell slipping down upon both knees, still stanchly clinging to the handle of the knife, which was thus twisted upwards. Cut to the quick, Bruin screamed again with anguish, and vibrated his paws, and gnashed his teeth, preliminary, as it seemed, to folding this new-found foe in a cruel embrace. Max felt the hot breath, and shrank in dread. But the blow had been well placed. Before its purpose could be carried out, the fatally wounded animal, staggering for an instant while its strength ebbed, fell sideways heavily, dragging Max with it. As it lifted its head once more to snap at its conqueror, Jack, who had got upon his feet, struck it vigorously a series of blows with the butt of the rifle. Then, with a great gasp, it died. To make matters sure, Jack bent over and cut its throat.

"Are you hurt?" he said earnestly, as Max picked himself up in a bewildered fashion.

"I don't think so. Is he dead?"

"Yes; but your jacket is torn. Your left hand is bleeding. Did he bite you?"

Max glanced at his sleeve, from underneath which some blood was trickling. "I think he grabbed me once with one of his paws, but it doesn't amount to much."

"O Max, Max, you saved my life! If it hadn't been for you, he'd have torn me to pieces. Take off your coat. Oh, I am so sorry!"

Max obeyed, smiling. "See, it is nothing," he said, exhibiting his bared arm, which was somewhat scratched, though not severely. "It is only on the surface. How I am trembling! My teeth are chattering."

"I should think they would. But you killed him. You're sure of the rifle now."

Jack had taken out his handkerchief, and was binding it round the wounded arm. "I thought I was a goner," he continued. "How his eyes glared! You *are* trembling, poor fellow, that's a fact. There, that'll hold, I guess. I wonder if I hit him."

They both stooped down to examine the prize. The bear was lying in a pool of blood. On rolling him over, the knife appeared sticking out a few inches below the heart, and there was another wound higher up, between the left breast and shoulder, which had been bleeding profusely.

"I did hit him," said Jack. "See," and he pointed to the orifice. "But he wouldn't have died from that, would he?"

"I don't know," said Max. "I know very little about bears."

"Except how to kill them. O Max, it's splendid! What will Colonel Russell say? Tell me, how did you feel? Did you think you were going to kill him?"

"I didn't have much time to think about anything. I don't understand how I managed to do it."

"Well, you did it; and you saved my life. The blade must have gone straight through his heart. Shall I pull it out?"

"If you like."

It was no very easy matter. Jack had to rest one foot on the body of the bear, and haul with a vim. "You're a great deal stronger than I thought you were, Max," he said, when he had drawn it out. "How much do you suppose this fellow weighs? He's fat as butter, isn't he? You know the skin's worth a lot, Max, if it's in good condition. I do hope it is."

"I'm glad I haven't got to kill him over again," said Max with a shiver, receiving and returning to its sheath the knife which Jack had been cleaning on the grass.

Jack looked at him in rather a puzzled manner. "It'll teach us one thing," he said, "and that is not to go about without spare cartridges in our pockets. Golly!" he added suddenly. "How dark it is getting!" This was certainly the case. In their excitement they had failed to notice that the sun had gone down, and that night was upon them.

"What are we to do?" said Max.

"We can't find our way back until to-morrow. We shall have to sleep here so far as I can see. Have you the least idea where we are?"

"Not the least."

"We must have tramped a good many miles," said Jack. "I hope this fellow's mate doesn't live anywhere near here. We'd better look round a little before we turn in."

It was not a bad place for a night's rest, thanks to the velvety moss which overspread the forest floor. After his cautionary speech, Jack had gone to examine the hollow tree, but found no signs of other bears. Apparently it had never been occupied.

"How about a fire?" asked Max, as Jack returned. "Have you any matches?"

"Jer-us-alem!" Jack fumbled anxiously in his pockets. All those in his coat and trousers he turned inside out to no purpose, and hope was rapidly on the wane, when his face suddenly became radiant, and he produced from his vest-pocket a single match.

"Hurrah!" he exclaimed.

"What luck!" said Max.

"One bullet and one match. Fine sportsmen we are. And if I don't turn the match to more account than I did the bullet, we shall have to go to bed supperless."

"I don't see but that we shall have to, any-way," said Max. "What is there to eat?"

"Eat? The bear, of course."

Max laughed. "I had forgotten him."

"Bear's meat is first rate, I believe. It'll save us from starving, at all events. We'd have been in a nice pickle if we had not killed him, even supposing we had not been inside of him."

By means of searching a little, the boys collected a considerable quantity of twigs and bark that would be serviceable for starting a fire, including some of the decayed wood torn off by Bruin. They came across a number of logs of more or less size within a small radius, so that ample material for a blaze was assured, provided that all went well at the start. Jack made a little pile, and, after altering its arrangement several times, said, holding out the match, —

"I want you to light it, Max."

"No, go ahead."

"I shall only make a mess of it." There was a decided touch of ruefulness in Jack's tone.

But Max shook his head. "I'd rather have you light it."

"You mustn't blame me, then, if it goes out." So saying, Jack, having critically ascertained the direction of the wind, set his back to it, and having taken off his hat, and dropped it in front of him, seized the match firmly, and struck it on a stone. Immediately he darted it within the hat, and bent down protectingly. It was an ordinary lucifer; and for a moment, as the ignited sulphur eat its way down the head, the boys held their breath. A flicker of blue fire followed, and the wood burst into flame. Still guarding it from the wind, Jack conveyed it in safety underneath the pile. Here there was another critical period. The bark and leaves seemed an eternity in catching. Jack held the blazing match until his fingers were smartly scorched, then tucked the remnant well into the midst of the heap. But it was already lighted, as the crackling of the dry twigs and the curling thread of smoke attested.

"Good enough, Jack," said Max.

To avoid all chances of a catastrophe, Jack fanned with his hat the mounting flame until the entire pile was in a roar.

"Now, if we're careful, she'll burn until morning," he said triumphantly.

The friendly blaze attractively lit up the gloom of night that had closed in upon them, opening vistas between the giant trees, bringing into prominence quaint protuberances on their sides, and mammoth toadstools springing from their roots. The boys were glad of the warmth, too, and stretched out their hands to the glow. Moreover, they were well nigh faint with hunger. Accordingly, as soon as the fire was roaring to his entire satisfaction, Jack got down on his knees, and attacked the carcass with his knife. As cooking utensils were lacking, the only feasible method of getting a square meal was to cut strips of meat, and spitting them on twigs expose them to the heat until they were palatable. The example thus set was speedily followed by Max, and the experiment proved diverting, as well as successful in the way of appeasing hunger. The fat meat sizzled until it frizzled, giving out an odor that suggested excellent ham. They cut scraps just large enough to be popped into their mouths when cooked, and delectable morsels many of them were. The neighboring brook supplied them with limpid water, so that as regards food and drink they felt highly content.

When their appetites were sated, they set to work collecting fire-wood, which, without an axe, required diligent wandering with torches. But a sufficient quantity for the night was procured at last. Then they composed themselves, with their backs against a large tree, and their feet extended towards the crackling logs, and discussed their plans for sleeping. In the absence of blankets or anything to lie on, it seemed more prudent to divide the night into watches, so that the fire should be kept alive. Besides, the idea that one of Bruin's family, or some other dangerous inhabitant of the forest, might be within prowling distance, made unguarded slumber seem less attractive than usual. By sleeping for two hours at a time, and being waked by his companion, each would be able to get a fair amount of unperturbed rest.

"I don't suppose there's really any danger, and I don't know that it would help much if one of us *were* awake, in case any creature should be inclined to attack us," said Max.

"We have our knives," answered Jack. "We should have a chance to get on our feet, at least. Besides, the big fire, and one of us sitting up with the rifle in his lap, would be likely to keep off any single animal. He wouldn't know that the gun wasn't loaded."

Careful search had enabled them, while collecting fuel, to discover some hemlock boughs. Of these they had broken off a sufficient number to make their couch less uncomfortable, and after freeing them from dew they spread them on what appeared the most desirable spot, under cover of the tree and close to the fire. Although Jack was anxious to give Max the first opportunity to sleep, Max insisted on drawing lots, which was done by tossing up a cent, — a very useless possession to have in one's pocket at such a time. The fates decided in accordance with Jack's desire; and he prepared for his two hours' vigil by sitting bolt upright, with his back to the tree, ready to cry " Who comes there?" at the least hint of peril. Max was asleep a moment or two after laying himself down, and the sentinel was left with his own thoughts and the sputtering fire as companions. At first his senses were completely on the alert. He listened intently, imagining every sound an indication of an approaching enemy, and that he saw animal shapes on the edge of the circle which divided the fire-light from the darkness. But the forest was noticeably still. Only occasionally did the cries of its inmates break the tranquillity, and there was no river to murmur. The snapping of the logs was rather a spur to drowsiness. Indeed, it was not long before Jack found his most serious concern to be keeping himself awake. He had literally to pinch his legs and arms. He felt too comfortable in every position he took. At last he gave a great start, realizing that there had been a gap in his consciousness. The fire had lost some of its brilliancy. How long had he slept? He looked at his watch, and found that it must have been, as well as he could judge, ten minutes. This was terrible. To sleep at one's post! What if a watchful wild-cat had taken advantage of these ten minutes to make a dart for Max? Could he ever have forgiven himself!

So tragically did this view of the case strike Jack, that he sprang up, and after replenishing the fire saw fit to promenade in front of it, rather than trust himself again in a recumbent position. This exercise served to drive away his tendency to sleep, so that when the two hours had elapsed he concluded not to wake Max, who was lying like a log. It was a glorious night overhead.

The moon had not yet risen, but the stars were clear and brilliant. He rehearsed the events of the day, and trembled once more at his own narrow escape. Somehow his feeling toward his companion had completely changed. He felt kindly, tenderly, in fact, toward him, and envied him not at all his certainty of winning the rifle. Jack did not put these sentiments into language, but he was vividly conscious of them. Such a place and time were well adapted for bringing him face to face with what he was, and giving the better part of his nature a chance to assert itself.

The breaking apart of a large log, which let the pile resting upon it fall into the fire with a loud sputter, disturbed his reverie, and caused Max to sit up straight and look at his watch.

"Why, Jack, it is one o'clock! You were to have waked me at twelve."

"Is it? You looked so comfortable I couldn't bear to disturb you."

"But that isn't fair," said Max. "You are just as tired as I, and need your sleep just as much."

"I'm not a bit sleepy." Jack squatted down beside him, and looked pensively at the flames.

" Have you heard or seen anything ? "

" No."

" Lie down, then, and shut your eyes, or you'll be used up to-morrow. We've got a hard tramp before us, lugging that bear."

Jack made no answer for a moment; then he said, " I want to beg your pardon, Max, before I go to sleep."

" For what, Jack ? "

" For everything; for — well, you know how I've treated you ever since we left home. I'd an idea at the start that you were — er — a tender-foot " —

" A what ? "

" A tenderfoot — er — sort of soft, and not very manly. Some of the others thought so, too. But you're the manliest and pluckiest of all of us, and the most of a sportsman, though you've not been used to roughing it as most of us have. Besides, I'd no more right than you to the first shot at the bear. I stole it. And I wish to tell you how sorry I am for being mean and disagreeable, and I hope you'll forgive me."

Once started, Jack spoke fluently, as though

the words were the genuine overflow of his
heart.

"Forgive you, Jack? Of course I will, if I've
anything to forgive," said Max pleasantly. "But
you were all of you right about me. I am a good
deal of a tenderfoot; at any rate, I was when
I started. I know nothing about games or anything that the rest of you are interested in;
and when I saw you all so strong and active and
clever, it mortified me terribly. I saw you
considered me like a girl, and I'll admit that some
of your jests made me feel badly; but I never
thought of blaming you for them, because I knew
they were deserved. But they spurred me on to
try to become more manly, and I'm glad if you
think I've succeeded. As for the bear, it was an
accident. I had to do something, for the next
moment he would have been eating you. But
I would have given a good deal at the time
if I could have run away."

"It isn't only the bear, it's everything," replied
Jack seriously. "You were ever so plucky in
that race the other day, and sensible, too. If I'd
been willing to rest as you did, I might have

passed you, and I knew that that was the proper thing to do, for I've been used to rowing; but I was obstinate, and so I got beaten. I've been thinking, too, that I could tire you out since we came up to the Narrows; and yet even if I'd been able to, which I haven't, it wouldn't have proved anything except that I was a bully."

"You judge yourself too harshly, Jack," Max interposed.

"No, I don't," he answered impetuously. "What have I to boast of, anyway? I'm tolerably strong and athletic, and all that, and I can row and play ball better than the average; but that's the whole. And only think what you can do, Max. You are a good scholar" —

"How do you know?"

"Mr. Holt says so. And you can speak no end of languages, and are fond of books. I make believe to despise books and poetry and such things; but I'm not so big a fool as not to envy those who are fond of them." Jack spoke as if he were glad to make a clean breast of his shortcomings.

"But you can do so many things I cannot,"

said Max. "Besides, it would be very easy for you to learn in a short time all I know about books."

"Could I?" asked Jack earnestly.

"I am sure you could. And it was very kind of you to speak so to me, Jack. I think we shall always be friends."

" There's my hand on it," said Jack, extending his brown fingers, which cordially returned the hearty pressure they received.

After this the boys were silent, and presently Jack dropped over on his side and fell asleep. Max watched patiently until two hours were passed, then waked him. By this time there were indications of approaching dawn, which cheered their hearts, and prompted Max to suggest that they dispense with the vigil. Jack, however, insisted on mounting guard again. At first he continued his promenade, and took further precautions against being caught napping by building up the fire; but as the light increased, beginning to feel weary, he concluded to sit down for a while. Although by struggling manfully he succeeded in keeping awake until it was broad day, his capacity for resisting temptation became exhausted at this point, and at five o'clock any stray animal might have helped itself to either of the young hunters without fear of interruption from the other. But if any such approached, it chose to confine its proceedings to inspection; for they slept long and well, until the sunbeams climbed up behind the tree-tops, and darted into their eyes. Jack was the first to awake, which he did with a great start, realizing at once what he had been guilty of. It was nine by his watch. With a sheepish air, which was tempered, however, by perceiving Max still motionless, he arose from his hard couch, and, after bathing his face and hands in the brook, built up anew the fire, and began to prepare breakfast, which, of course, would have to consist of more strips of bear's meat. By the time that a number of these were duly sizzling, his companion regained consciousness, but revealed so bewildered and woebegone a visage when the truth dawned upon him, that Jack burst into laughter.

"Why, Jack, it's nearly half-past nine. Why didn't you wake me?"

Max's tone betrayed so much mortification, that Jack confessed, after pretending for a few moments that he had been awake since daybreak, the real state of the case. Then they had another hearty laugh together over their joint incapacity as sentinels; though Jack declared himself really the one at fault in that he had failed to call Max at the end of the third two hours because asleep himself. But Max insisted that there was no excuse for his having slept six hours on a stretch.

The boys were not quite so enthusiastic over the breakfast as they had been over their supper. Perhaps now that the novelty of dropping bits of meat into their mouths from a twig had worn off, they would have been willing to return to more civilized methods. Nevertheless, they ate enough to satisfy hunger, and then rose the important question as to how what remained of Bruin should be transported to where they had left the canoe. But, to begin with, neither felt by any means ready to guarantee that he would be able to find the canoe, or indeed the river. Beyond the fact that they had crossed the brook, they were considerably in the dark to as the route by which they had reached their present encampment. To retrace their steps by means of the bear's tracks, suggested itself as a shrewd plan, but on investigation these seemed to have disappeared. Discouraged thereby, they concluded, after lugging for a few hundred yards the bear's body, suspended between them from a pole which they had picked up, to leave the carcass, and return for it later. So, as best they could, they scooped out a hole with their knives, into which they put Bruin, covering him with leaves, moss, and stones. They had already cooked, and stuffed into their pockets, a sufficient portion of the flesh to save them from fasting during the day. Then they marked a tree in a peculiar fashion, to indicate the neighborhood of his resting-place, and started on their journey, blaizing the forest to right and left from time to time as they proceeded.

Jack had a general idea of where the river lay with regard to the points of the compass, as indicated by the sun, and they kept along in accordance with his admonitions. But the way seemed wholly unfamiliar to them, as indeed it must, unless they had been fortunate enough to return by exactly the same course that they had come, which was improbable, if for no other reason, because they had traveled in a zigzag manner while pursuing the bear. Although there was something ludicrous to them in the situation, the prospect of wandering about the woods indefinitely was by no means agreeable, and there was no absolute certainty that they were not getting deeper and deeper into the forest every minute. A glimpse of two caribou served only to increase their fears, as they had been told that deer were rarely met with near the river. At noon, it became hot. They stopped for luncheon, feeling completely at a loss as to their whereabouts. Jack exercised his lungs by holloaing a number of times out of sheer desperation, thinking, perhaps, that by some lucky chance they might have wandered within hearing of the rest of the party. They hoped, too, by listening, to detect the rush of the river, but the woods were as still as the grave.

"It doesn't matter much which way we go. It's

all luck where we come out," said Jack, when they were ready to start again.

"Not if your theory about the sun is correct. It provokes me to think that I haven't the least idea as to whether it was shining on our backs or in our faces yesterday afternoon."

"I thought I was sure about it. But you see where we are. It has all the look of the forest primeval. Hollo-o-o-o-a," Jack cried again vociferously. "No use," he continued, after listening intently for some minutes. "We sha'n't starve, anyway, for another twenty-four hours; and the best way is to leg it as fast as we can, and trust to coming out somewhere."

Acting on this suggestion, they tramped along in a straight line for another two hours, Jack leading the way. They traversed whatever lay in the path, be it thicket, bramble, bush, or morass. Their clothes were fuzzy and prickly with burrs and briars. If it had been of any use to complain, they would have acknowledged themselves footsore and weary. But to all appearances, when they came to a halt once more, in order to recover breath and listen for the river, they were just as far from it as ever. The sun was getting down again behind the tree-tops, and the vistas ahead looked gloomy.

" What had we better do ? " said Max.

"Keep on, it seems to me. It means kill or cure."

" I am beginning to be reminded of the babes in the wood. 'The robins so red brought strawberry leaves, and over them spread.' "

" I don't believe there are either robins or strawberry leaves in this wilderness. Wild-cats and toadstools will do our business. Are you ready to go on ? "

" Oui, monsieur."

Lightly as they seemed to regard their plight, it was undeniably getting serious. By husbanding the supply of bear's meat, they would have food enough for the night and part of another day ; but supposing that they were tramping in the wrong direction, might they not go on indefinitely without arriving anywhere until they should literally starve? Since they had journeyed in vain for one day, might they not do the same for another and still another?

If such thoughts occurred to the boys, they did not put them into words, but still struggled onward, keeping up their spirits, as the afternoon shadows deepened, with cheerful talk.

"Hard luck, wasn't it, that we should get within range of those caribou, and not be able to fire at them?" said Jack. "One might trot up and peep into the barrel of this gun with perfect safety, if he only knew it."

"We should have had to bury them, though, just as we did the bear, if we had got them. For my part, I feel more inclination for a swallow of water than for anything else just now."

"Then gratify your wish," said Jack. Curiously enough, as Max spoke, he had caught sight of a small brook, the first that they had met with since morning. After delaying here long enough to slake their thirst, and bathe their faces, they plunged forward again, intent upon making as much progress as they could before dark. Half an hour later Jack suddenly stopped short, and called attention to a plant, one branch of which was hanging down half broken, as though some one had stepped upon it.

"Who could have done that?" he asked.

Together they examined it by the twilight. "It must have been done by one of us yesterday," said Max presently, in answer to the question.

"Whoever did it must have been coming from there," continued Jack, indicating a direction almost at right angles with that in which they had been travelling; "for, you see, it is bent down this way."

"You clever creature! That seems likely, now that you mention it, but I should never have thought of it myself."

Jack had stepped beyond the crushed plant, and was endeavoring to make out if there were any other similar indications; but he could find none, and it was too dark to decipher footprints.

"We'd better follow this for a little," he said. "It will do no harm, anyway.

Spurred by hope, they had tramped on in this new direction for about fifteen minutes, when Jack stopped again, and exclaimed eagerly, —

"Listen, Max, do you hear anything?"

Max obeyed. "It sounds like the rush of water."

"It's the river!"

"Hooray!"

"We're not out of the woods yet," said Jack, whom adversity was making cautious. But he dashed forward at a lively jog, nevertheless, stopping every few moments to listen anew.

More and more distinct grew the sound, changing hope to security, until at last, when they had run quarter of a mile, their eyes were delighted by a glimpse that set their hearts bounding still faster.

"It's the Falls!" they exclaimed together in amazement, as they came out on the bank.

So it certainly was. A hundred yards below where they were standing the picturesque cascade was leaping and tumbling into the river. They could only see its crest, but they had no doubt as to its identity. The last glow of the sunset lingered on the water, and the sky was radiant with promise for the morrow. The boys, glad to be free from uncomfortable fears of being lost, sat down on a stump to enjoy the tranquil scene. It was half-past eight o'clock. Another quarter of an hour's walk down stream would bring them to

where they had left their canoe, and it seemed
advisable to pass the rapid below the Narrows
before it became pitch dark. They found sitting
down, however, so agreeable, that the dusk was
nearly darkness before they got upon their legs
again. They were in the best of spirits. Such
an adventure as theirs they felt to be one that
would make the others green with envy.

CHAPTER VIII.

" INJUN FALLS."

JACK and Max, with the day's experience fresh in mind, took care not to lose sight of the river as they pursued their way to reach the canoe. By the time they were close to where they had left it, night had overspread the sky. The stars were burning quietly and with no especial lustre, so that it was pretty dark. But owing to the peculiar shape of the pool, which widened out so noticeably from the jaws of "the narrow place," as the guides were wont to call it, they found no difficulty in fixing the spot. There lay the canoe, bottom up, just as she had been left by them more than twenty-four hours before.

Jack, who was in advance, had stooped down to examine her, when Max touched him on the shoulder, whispering at the same moment, —

" Do you see that ? "

Jack looked. At the lower end of the pool, close to the other bank, was what seemed to be a low, flickering light. " What do you make it out to be?" he asked, in a tone of awe. " It's too small for a fire.   See, it is moving this way."

As Jack spoke, the mysterious manifestation glided a few feet out into the pool, and then immediately darted back again.

" They may be hunting for us," said Max.

"But they wouldn't have missed us so soon. Besides, why should any one be prowling round at night in that fashion, if they were?   There are no signs of a camp on the shore."

" You remember what I saw the other night? " said Max, after a pause.

" You mean the canoe? " asked Jack, in rather an uneasy tone.   " What of that? "

" Nothing — only — if there is such a thing as an *ignis fatuus* " —

" A what? "

" An *ignis fatuus* — will-of-the-wisp — whatever one chooses to call it.   I don't believe there are such things.   And yet, what can that be? "

" It isn't imagination, anyway," whispered Jack

decidedly. "A light's a light, and we both can see it with our two eyes."

"Would it do to hail it?"

"No, no. Let's wait and see what it does. Look, it is moving again."

The boys had instinctively crouched down behind the boat, so as to see without being seen in case of necessity. The strange illumination now began to move steadily forward, until it reached the middle of the pool; then of a sudden it flashed up, seeming to be lifted from the water.

"Je — hos — aphat!" whispered Jack, in rather a relieved tone. "I believe it's a torch, and that there's a real canoe with some one in it."

"Who can it be?"

"Give it up. Don't you see the outline?"

"Yes, yes."

Jack's explanation was evidently the correct one. The increased brightness of the flame disclosed the distinct though dusky shadow of a skiff, controlled by a single figure. Obviously the individual, whoever he was, had just fastened the torch at the bow in such a manner that it extended over the water. The eyes of the boys, grown more accustomed to the night, could discern him now standing up and peering into the pool. Before him he held something which they assumed to be a paddle. What could it mean? What was this mysterious individual doing in the middle of the river at such an hour.

The wonder which was holding them mute was broken by Jack.

"Why didn't we think of it before? It's Pete Labouisse, of course."

"I shouldn't be surprised," whispered Max, in a tone of conviction. "He's after fish, I suppose."

"He's flambeauing, and it's against the law. I wish the Colonel were here."

Just then they perceived a swirl on the surface of the water underneath the flame of the torch, and simultaneously the figure in the canoe darted forward the implement in his hand. There followed a vigorous splashing, and they were able to distinguish that a huge salmon was being lifted over the gunwale.

"The villain!" exclaimed Jack. "He speared the poor creature. Did you see?"

"HE'S FLAMBEAUING, AND IT'S AGAINST THE LAW." — P 300.

"Isn't there any way to prevent him?" asked Max indignantly.

"We could frighten him off for the time being. But wouldn't it be better to wait and see if we can't get even with him somehow?" The suggestion, though vague, was so far satisfactory to Max that he replied with earnestness, —

"If only we could!"

The noise of further splashing was audible. The Indian had taken another fish. His system was simple enough. The vivid reflection of the torch in the black water lured the poor salmon up from the depths, and as they reached the surface his lance was hurled with deadly precision into their brains. While the boys sat straining their eyes in following his movements, Pete continued his operations with success, filching salmon after salmon from the pool, over which he glided noiselessly. This went on for more than an hour. Nursing their wrath, and yet uncertain what to do, Jack and Max watched him without interruption. When the pool had become thoroughly stirred up by the futile struggles of the victims to escape, the marauder paddled to the opposite bank again. After remaining there some little time, — apparently, as well as the boys could make out, for the purpose of depositing his catch, — he sallied forth again, and passed on up river.

"He's going for the other pools, I guess," said Jack.

The boys now held a council of war. The first idea that occurred to them was to get possession of the salmon already slaughtered, in case Pete had left them on the other side. Therefore they launched their canoe as noiselessly as possible, and, after waiting until the glimmer of the torch had vanished in the distance, stole across the pool. On reaching the opposite bank, they disembarked again, and finding nothing on the shore began to grope among the bushes. It was very dark, and their lack of matches was bothersome. But at last Max gave a low cry of satisfaction. He had discovered the whole hoard of fish underneath the shadow of a pine, and covered with alder-bushes. With eager fingers the boys took possession of them, and brought them down to the water's edge. There were fifteen salmon in all. Jack and Max were bitter in their denunciation of the cruel butchery.

"What perfect beauties!" said Max. "See — see this fellow; and here's one larger still."

"Regular whales. Those two must weigh at least forty pounds each. It's a diabolical outrage."

"It's murder — midnight assassination; that's the name for it. There are three or four fish among them bigger than anything we've caught yet."

"I know it," groaned Jack. "And we might have caught them to-morrow. What let's do with them?"

This was a serious question, and required thought.

"Suppose we run them down in the canoe, and stow them in the icehouse," Max suggested. "Pete would never dare to come after them there."

Jack assented to this plan. The prospect of reaching camp again added attraction to the scheme, for, though excited, they were well-nigh worn out with fatigue and lack of sleep. They had eaten nothing but cold bear's meat all day.

"How good a slice of one of those fellows would taste!" said Max, as they were lifting the noble fish into the canoe.

"I wouldn't eat one to — to save myself from starvation," exclaimed Jack fiercely. "They've had no chance for their lives, poor creatures, and we've no right to eat them."

"I ought to have thought of that. What, though, can be done with them, if we don't eat them?" continued Max, after a moment.

This was rather a poser. "Bury them — or burn them. *I* don't mean to eat them, anyway," said Jack, by way of settling the matter so far as he was concerned.

The fifteen fish made a heavy freight; and running the rapid at the Narrows was a decidedly ticklish affair, requiring the utmost caution on the part of Jack, who was in the bow, to avoid disaster. This passed in safety, their course down river was comparatively smooth, though necessarily slow on account of the darkness. The boys chuckled gaily at the thought of the anger and astonishment which the half-breed would experience on discovering the loss of his splendid mess of fish. On arrival at the camp, having hastily consigned their cargo to the ice-house, and taken off the edge of hunger by means of pilot bread and some pieces of chocolate, they had to consider what their next move should be; for they were agreed to balk Pete, if possible, of his entire night's haul. All sense of fatigue was forgotten.

On reflection, the most sure plan seemed to be that they should pole up again to the pool at the Narrows, in the hope of forestalling Pete's arrival. They could there lie in ambush, and be governed in their actions by circumstances. Accordingly they set off, well supplied this time with cartridges, matches, and food, so as to be prepared for every emergency. When they reached the entrance to the pool, there was no appearance of the torch or canoe. All was dark and still. Stealing cautiously along the shore, the boys landed at the spot where they had discovered the salmon, and on investigation found that Pete had apparently not yet returned, for there were no more fish concealed in the bushes. Jack then suggested that they cross over to their former hiding-place and keep watch.

Here they remained patiently for about half an hour without hearing or seeing anything of interest. It was then nearly three o'clock in the morning. Max had dropped off into a doze, and Jack was beginning to ask himself whether Pete could have got wind of them and slipped away, when suddenly there appeared above the tree-tops across the river a strange light in the sky that made him think that the sun was rising. But a moment's thought convinced him that it was too early. What did the light mean, then? Were the woods on fire? While he was wondering if this could be the case, the illumination deepened into golden sheen, and a few moments later the fiery half moon rose into sight, lighting up the surface of the river. Absorbed by the changed aspect of the night, Jack was startled to perceive the long anticipated canoe glide suddenly down into the pool, headed for the opposite shore. The torch was no longer burning, but it was easy in the moonlight to make out the half-breed paddling in the stern. His skiff rode deep in the water, as though heavily laden.

Jack roused Max, and whispered to him that

Pete was going to land. With keen excitement they watched him, just after stepping ashore, stoop and scrutinize the ground, look about him as though suspicious, and then ascend the bank without unloading his canoe.

"He has noticed our tracks," said Jack. "What had we better do? Do you suppose we could slip across and cut loose his canoe before he could get back?"

"It would be risky, for if we were to fail he might make it hot for us," said Max.

"We are two to his one."

Pete's reappearance at this moment decided the matter. He came stealing back like an angry cat, glancing furtively to right and left and across the river, in such a way that the boys held their breath, and slunk down as much as possible behind their canoe. He had evidently discovered his loss, and was apprehensive of danger. He threw the painter into his skiff, leaped inside, and seized the paddle.

"What let's do?" asked Jack feverishly.

"He's going down river," replied Max, without answering the question.

"If he gets a start on us, we shall never catch him. Let's follow him, Max, and try to get the fish."

"Whatever you say, Jack. I'm ready."

Pete was by this time at the head of the rapid. Spryly, but seeking to be noiseless, the boys sprang up, and pushed their boat into the water.

"Will you go bow, Max?" Jack asked, willing to renounce the post of responsibility.

"No, no. You paddle much better than I."

"All right." Jack darted forward, and took his position. "Are you ready?"

"Go ahead."

A half-dozen strokes sent them to the verge of the rapid, mid-way in which their enemy was visible tossing on the angry water. It was no longer dark. There was a sort of twilight. The effulgence of the old moon was mingled with the first indications of dawn. As yet Pete had not perceived that he was followed. He was moving with no especial swiftness, being intent apparently on steering clear of the dangerous boulders in the rapid, which might readily knock a hole in a canoe so much below the surface. Behind him his pursuers made all the haste that was consistent with safety, appreciating that it was important to take advantage of every moment before they should be observed.

Was it intuition, habitual dread, or some detected noise that caused the Indian to turn his head just as he had reached the foot of the rapid? It might well have been the last, for not more than a dozen yards of foaming water separated him from his pursuers at the moment. As he realized the situation, they could not discern the expression of his face. He uttered no cry, made no gesture; simply turned his head, and plied his paddle with all his might and skill.

"Now for it, Max," cried Jack. "Let's go for him."

"Look out; snub her."

"Yes, I see."

The canoe ahead was gliding forward at a wonderful rate; and, not to lose the advantage they had already gained, they could not afford to be too prudent. There was only a few feet of dangerous water left. This safely passed, the river was smooth and safe.

"Snub her, Jack, snub her," Max yelled, as he heard the canoe grind her nose, and felt himself tilted to one side so that the water almost poured in over the edge.

"All right, Max."

It was a close shave; but skillful manipulation of the paddle had swept them past the point of danger, and brought them into a swift, unimpeded current. They had lost a little on their enemy, yet not materially; and had they not four arms to his two? To be sure, he was an Indian, accustomed all his days to paddling and to this river; but, on the other hand, his canoe being full of fish was unfit to be handled rapidly by one man.

On they went, neither canoe gaining on the other, the consciousness of which doubtless caused Pete every few moments to dart a glance behind him, and afterwards to ply his paddle still more rapidly through the water. But the boys, too, having settled down to their work, were sending their canoe spinning forward in famous fashion. Another rapid was reached, and encountered successfully; and then they came in sight of the log-cabin, past which they glided so swiftly, that, ere they realized where they were, they had left it behind. Still on, and neither canoe gaining, neither losing.

Of a sudden the blade of Pete's paddle breaks in his hand, serving to divert the canoe somewhat from her course, and then to check her while the Indian reaches forward for another which he happens to have. Every foot is precious, and by means of this misadventure the pursuers have gained ground. Moreover, the new paddle is a smaller, frailer one, ill suited for the strenuous work that it must do in order that its owner may maintain the lead. He evidently appreciates this, for, beside looking behind him still more frequently, he glances now and again from right to left as though scanning the banks. High cliffs tower on either side for the most part, up which any one seeking to climb must have the legs and facility of a fly to be successful. But doubtless the wily half-breed, acquainted with every foot of the river, knows of places where the precipice rises more gradually, affording to one who is cat-like and sinewy opportunities for escape by swinging from a tree to a ledge, and thence to some other shelter, until the height is won.

The boys are quick to appreciate his intention. They would like nothing better than that he should abandon canoe, fish, and all, and take to the woods. Their triumph would then be complete. With the idea of accelerating this apparent disposition on the part of their enemy to take refuge in flight, Jack cries to Max, —

"Hand me the gun."

"You're not going to fire at him, surely, Jack?"

"Only over his head, to scare him. It may drive him ashore."

Max drops his paddle, and deftly reaches forward the rifle. For an instant their headway is checked, while Jack, putting the butt to his shoulder, aims deliberately many yards wide of Pete's body, and pulls the trigger. The sharp report echoes through the hills, while the Indian turns with a look that is half terror and half menace, and utters something that sounds jargon to the boys.

"Do you suppose he has a gun?" says Max.

"I guess not. Anyhow, he wouldn't dare to use it, for he would have to hang if he shot us."

The discharge does not seem to produce the result expected. On the contrary, as a consequence of it, and another which Jack has recourse to a moment later, Pete seems to change his mind in regard to escaping by means of the bank. Doubtless he fears that while seeking to do so he might more easily be pierced by a rifle-ball, for he naturally imagines that the shots fired at him are intended to kill. On he dashes, crouching low in the canoe, and preferring to trust to outstripping his opponents on the water, while the east breaks into shafts of light that make the moon paler and blot out the stars.

All at once Jacks starts, and exclaims almost with horror, "Hark! We're nearly at the Injun Falls. I'd forgotten them."

"So we must be. I can hear the roar," answers Max. "What shall we do, Jack?"

"What'll he do?"

"Do you suppose he'll try to run them?"

"He's likely to come to grief if he does."

It was evident now, from the manner in which

Pete was straining every nerve to keep his lead, that he, too, had recognized the murmur of the dangerous cascade ahead, and was hoping to devise therefrom some means of escape.

A moment more brought them in sight of the foaming rapid, through which only the most skillful canoemen could hope to pass in safety. Pete, as he reached the border of the crested, churning whirlpool, looked behind him once more, and, regarding his hunters with a smile of malice, beckoned them on. If they wished his scalp, they must follow where he chose to lead. Would they dare to do so? Or if they did, would they, mere striplings as they were, be able to avoid being upset in the midst of the rapid? And disaster there meant not merely a wetting. The stoutest swimmer might well lose nerve and consciousness in that mad current, and be swept like a feather over the tawny Indian Falls.

"Shall we keep on?" asked Jack, looking back with flashing eyes. The idea of Pete's escaping through their unwillingness to follow, was galling; but, whatever his own sentiments might be, Max must be consulted.

"I'll do whatever you say, Jack."

"Come on, then."

No more was said. In another second the canoe was battling with the wild torrent but a few yards behind the desperate Indian's. Haste, indeed anything but deliberate, Argus-eyed caution, would assure destruction. To pick one's way zigzag through a labyrinth of cruel rocks, was the only chance for a safe passage.

"We'd better take to the poles," said Max. "We can hold her better if we do."

This was sound advice, and the example to do so had already been set them by Pete. Laying aside their paddles, they stood up over the frowning water, and gripped the bottom with the iron sockets seeking an avenue. The boiling surf made Jack feel giddy. To keep his balance, and at the same time chose a path through the hell-gate, was no easy matter. In front the other canoe was plunging madly, taxing to the uttermost the skill of the half-breed, who stood a little forward of the middle to keep her bow from swinging. Jack ducked his head that he might rub with his sleeve his eyes, which were so full of

spray, caused by the constant spattering, that
he could scarcely see, and at the same moment
the canoe bumped savagely against a rock.
He fairly staggered, and in saving himself from
falling overboard let in a quantity of water.
Bumping past the rock, the nose of the canoe
jammed itself in between two boulders, in a sort
of gully where the water ran like a mill-race and
plunged forward in a small cascade at the end.
They were fast stuck, and in such a way that
the bow projected over the declivity at a decidedly
disagreeable angle.　To extricate her without
coming to grief more seriously, was the work of
some moments, during which the boys nursed
the bitter consciousness that Pete was gaining on
them.　At last, after having taken in a quart or
two more water, they were free and dashing once
more as fast as they dared toward the dreaded
falls.　Pete had passed through three-fourths of
the rapid, and they were not far behind.　Would
he dare to take the leap?　Would they dare to
follow him if he did?　The tumult of the river
made their brains whirl, making it impossible
almost to think, much less to talk.　With eyes

fixed intently on the boiling water, with every sinew strained, they plied their poles, not knowing what would be the outcome, not seeking to anticipate it.

Just then Pete's canoe gave a sudden cant, owing doubtless to contact with some concealed rock, which threw the half-breed off his feet down upon the flooring, and buried her gunwale well under water.

"See, see! cried Jack, in almost agonized accents.

The deeply freighted canoe remained for a moment at a critical angle, as if hesitating whether to tip over, then slowly righted herself. Pete was on his feet again, using his pole vigorously, but unable to prevent her from exposing her flank to the current, which twisted and thwarted her course so completely, that before he could bring her head round Jack was thundering but a length or two behind, —

"Give us back those fish. You stole those fish."

The spectacle of his enemy's plight had prompted the boy to suggest terms that might, he thought, appeal to the fleeing Indian, and thus avert more serious consequences while there was still time. Pete turned his head at the outcry.

"Give us back the fish, and we'll let you go," repeated Jack, unable to believe that Pete would dare to take the leap, and confident that the salmon-spearer's only choice was between surrender and destruction.

But his words seemed only to spur on to more determined efforts the Indian, who, having brought the head of his half-sunken canoe into position once more, sent her driving forward, headed straight for the roaring cataract.

"Great Cæsar's ghost! he's going to run it."

As he spoke, Pete turned again, smiling and beckoning as he had done before, and then gave vent to another jargon utterance, that sounded like a note of triumph. He intended to go over the fall. There could be no doubt of it; for now it was too late for him to avoid doing so, whatever his desire might be. He was crouching low in the canoe, having exchanged, at the moment that he had emitted his challenge, his pole for his paddle, and had directed her into the middle of the stream where the current was swiftest.

Close behind, not more than half a dozen yards distant, came his pursuers, growing conscious, as they perceived that rocks no longer impeded them, that they too were on a down slope, and moving with terrible velocity. What was to be done? Should they follow? Not a word was spoken until Jack said suddenly, —

"Get your paddle out."

An instant later he gave a great gasp. He had seen the rival canoe give a wild leap into the air and disappear. For an instant a sickening sensation of dread took possession of him, and he would fain have turned aside. But it was impossible now. He felt himself being swept down a terrible smooth slide of water, that made him think of pale green glass.

"Hold tight, Max; we're going over," he uttered. Then for an instant a huge foaming gulf yawned below him, and he knew that they were pitching downward. He shut his eyes, and gripped his paddle like a vise. There was a moment of ghastly stillness, which seemed like

an eternity, and then he felt the canoe strike the
surface with a force that drove the water over
him in clouds. He knew that floods were pouring
into her, and that he was well-nigh submerged;
and yet before he could decide what had happened, the worst seemed to be over, for her nose
had reappeared above water. With a quick
glance behind him, he realized that they had
escaped serious injury. Max, pale as a ghost and
nearly as wet as he, sat in the stern unharmed,
though the canoe was full half-way to the brim.
Well behind them was the terrible cataract, on
the impetus from whose swift deluge they were
still being borne along at a mad rate. All this
Jack understood in an instant; and appreciating
that they had made the leap in safety, his next
thought was for Pete. As he looked forward
again, he beheld almost abreast of him in the
foam-flecked turbulent river a human figure,
wildly and vainly struggling to obtain a foothold.
Of the other canoe there was no vestige. There
was only to be seen a black head and gesticulating
pair of arms, which suddenly disappeared as the
victim's feet were deprived even of a passing

"HOLD TIGHT, MAX; WE'RE GOING OVER.'—P. 321.

contact with the slippery rocks at the bottom, owing to the increased depth of the galloping water, which now rolled him over and over, bringing him to the surface in another moment several yards beyond, a confused, gasping mass, uttering cries of terror, imploring help.

"He'll drown, he'll drown!" Jack heard Max exclaim in a tone of horror. The same thought was in his own mind. Evidently the half-breed could not swim, and was at the mercy of the rapid current. His desire for retaliation had been fully sated by the severe punishment which his enemy had already suffered in the loss of canoe and fish. Both the purloining of the loon and the flambeaning were amply avenged; and the idea of Pete's being drowned, as a result of the effort to recapture the salmon, struck him as terrible. What could he do to save him?

Instantly he plied his paddle, in the hope of catching up with the unfortunate struggler, in which attempt he was sturdily seconded by Max; but their canoe was so water-logged as to be nearly unmanageable. Jack realized, moreover, that if they were to bring it within grasping distance of the drowning man, they were certain to be upset. The half-breed, who was bravely struggling to keep his head above the surface, turned toward him a ghastly face full of despair, and reached out his arms as though begging for assistance.

"What can we do, Max?" Jack cried.

"We must save him somehow, or he will drown before our eyes."

Just then Pete went under for a second time, uttering a choking cry as he sank. With an impulsive movement Jack pulled his shirt over his head, and kicked off his shoes.

"Look out for her, Max, and follow me close."

"You mustn't, Jack, you mustn't! You can't do anything against that current."

Max's words of protest were cut short by a splash. Jack had leaped from the canoe into the river. He had resolved to save Pete, if possible. He was a good swimmer for his years, and he believed that he was equal to the emergency. If he could only keep clear of rocks, he felt sure that he should not be overcome by the current. These thoughts had been in his mind

as he jumped, and he had selected an unob-
structed, deep-looking spot into which to plunge.
As he emerged, he perceived Pete, who had
reappeared at the same moment. Fortunately
the half-breed was nearly unconscious, or he might
have questioned the motive of his pursuer in
seizing him. Remembering from what he had
read of the tendencies of drowning people, to
avoid being gripped in turn, Jack managed to
get his right arm under one of Pete's, in such
a way as to keep the half-breed's head above
water, and then tried to strike out for the shore.
He was conscious of being swept along by a
tremendous power, which twisted his legs about
in an alarming fashion, and prevented him from
moving otherwise than in the same way with it.
Plainly he was going down stream at a tremendous
pace. But fortunately again, the river, though
swift, continued deep, and only once did he come
in painful contact with the rocks. Before he
could collect himself, however, after grasping his
burden, he had been swept forward fifty yards.

Not far behind them followed Max, managing
with his paddle as best he could the unwieldy

canoe, which had swung across the stream, and was wobbling alarmingly. He kept his eyes fixed on the valiant rescuer, eager to afford him aid, and yet uncertain how to do so.

"I'm coming, Jack, I'm coming!" he shouted.

Another fifty yards was passed, and the dead weight of the unconscious Indian was beginning to pull Jack down. His own chin was barely above the water. Still he managed to keep Pete's face from being submerged, and did his best, while being carried on, to make some little progress toward the shore with his unencumbered right arm. Swift as the current continued, it was less rapid than at first; and hopes of being able to touch the bottom, and gain a foothold, buoyed up his courage. But he was fagged, and he ached. Several times the idea of letting his burden go, and saving himself, occurred to him, but still he held on.

At last, just as he felt that in another moment his strength would be exhausted, one of his feet, which were dragging lightly, touched a rock. Trusting that a little farther toward the shore the water might not be over his head, he made one vigorous endeavor to escape from the mid-stream, and succeeded so far that he found, on sinking both legs, that he was on the bottom, though the river was still up to his lips. The next instant the undertow deprived him of this advantage; but while treading water, he launched himself again toward the bank, and this time got a foothold where he was under water only as far as his chin. But, owing to the great difficulty of keeping Pete's face above the surface while in this process, he slipped and fell, so that he and the drowning man went completely under. But here again fortune favored him, in that he fell toward the shore. He managed to pick himself up again, and to recover, by dint of both hands, the still senseless half-breed. The river was now only up to his arm-pits; and, by planting his feet firmly apart, he was able to resist the current sufficiently to look about him. In another instant, Max was at his side with the canoe. Using the edge of this as a means of steadying himself, he reached a place where it was only up to his knees, then staggered to the bank, dragging Pete with him, and dropped exhausted on the beach. Max shot the canoe ashore, and got on his knees beside him. Jack had shut his eyes, but he opened them, and asked, —

"Is he drowned?"

"I don't know; I wanted to be sure you were not hurt."

"I'm all right. Look after Pete," Jack murmured faintly.

Max turned his attention to the Indian, who lay on his back, pale and apparently dead. But, as Max bent over him in horrible uncertainty, Pete gave a perceptible sigh.

"No, I think he's alive, thank God!" Max cried; and, though he had rather a vague idea as to the proper treatment for nearly drowned people, he began vigorously to rub the half-breed's hands.

"Turn him over on his face," said Jack; and he sat up himself, with the desire of helping his friend, but sank back again exhausted.

"Don't stir. I can do everything," cried Max beseechingly. "If you'll tell me what to do, I'll do it. A nice sort of fellow I am to come into the woods," he added, in disgust at his own ignorance.

Jack, who knew something about such matters, gave the necessary directions, and almost immediately was able to rise and superintend the process. After a few moments of rubbing, Pete gave unmistakable signs of coming to life. Max, who had pulled off his patient's boots, noticed, in chafing his feet, that he groaned whenever his right leg was disturbed. Apparently, it was severely hurt. At last, after a copious amount of water had trickled out of his mouth, and his skin had become tolerably warm, Pete opened his eyes. For an instant he looked dazed and alarmed at the sight of the two boys bending over him, and he made an effort as though to spring up; but the exertion destroyed his reviving consciousness. When, a moment or two later, he came to himself again, he regarded his captors with a half-sullen, half-astonished stare, apparently realizing what had happened, and at a loss to understand such magnanimity.

"Feel better?" Jack inquired, as the half-breed moved his head a little.

"Ya," was the guttural answer.

"Pretty close call you had."

This idiom was obviously beyond Pete's intelligence. He stared stupidly, and in another moment evinced a disposition to rise, which was not interfered with. But, as he was attempting to get on his feet, he suddenly groaned with pain, and sank upon the ground.

"What's the matter?" the boys cried together.

Pete's face had assumed the look of a desperate wounded animal. There was fury as well as the symptoms of suffering in his eyes. Lifting himself upon his elbow, he reached behind him, searching evidently for his knife; but Max, while restoring him, had removed, and tossed to one side, the belt to which it was attached. Still angrier in consequence of being thus foiled, he sprang up with the crafty elasticity. of a wild-cat, and made a leap for Jack's neck. Jack, astonished, stepped hastily backwards; and his would-be assailant pitched headlong, and lay on his face writhing.

The boys looked at each other in amazement for a moment, then Jack exclaimed, "That's a queer sort of return to make for having saved your life. I'm sorry if you're hurt, but you'd have been drowned if I hadn't jumped in after you."

Max at the same time picked up the belt and knife.

Pete made no answer, but lay groaning. It was evident he could not stand.

"I guess he must have broken his leg," said Jack presently. "I wonder what we'd better do with him."

"We can't be more than a mile and a half from the Big Salmon Hole," said Max.

"Let's ask him what he'd like us to do."
Max nodded.

"See here, your name's Pete Labouisse, isn't it?" Jack began, stooping over the half-breed, but careful to be on his guard against any sudden clutch.

Pete looked up, and scowled. "Ya, ya," he muttered.

"I thought I recognized you. I want to say that we're ready to help you in any way we can, only you must treat us as friends, and not jump at our throats as you did just now. Your canoe sank, I think, for there isn't any sign of her anywhere."

"Strike rock."

"That accounts for it. Well, if you say so, we'll take you in ours down to where our friends are. They sha'n't hurt you," Jack added, noticing Pete's look of alarm at this suggestion. "You've had punishment enough already for spearing our fish."

The Indian blinked, and looked rather nonplussed. Such generosity was novel to him. Presumably he doubted its genuineness.

"What do you say? Shall we take you with us?"

"I stay here. You go,' answered Pete.

"But you'll starve," interposed Max.

"Isn't your leg broken?" Jack asked. "If it is, you ought to have a doctor look at it. You needn't be afraid," he continued, divining Pete's suspicions. "We'll neither of us tell tales on you, so no one will be able to put you in prison."

The lad's tone and manner were so reassuring, that, in spite of this allusion to possible legal complications, the Indian's expression softened a little. The idea of being left alone to shift for himself in his present crippled condition was not agreeable.

"Get ready the canoe, Max. We ourselves ought to start, anyway."

"You take me Basin?" queried Pete at this moment.

"Where? Oh, Gaspé Basin! Yes, if it's necessary."

The prisoner shook his head repugnantly.

"We're going to take you to the camp at the Big Salmon Hole first; that's only a mile below, you know. When you're cured, you can go to the Basin or not as you prefer," said Jack.

"Ya, ya. I go with you."

"All right."

"That's first-rate," said Max, who had tipped the water out of the canoe by this time. When all was ready, the boys signified to Pete that if he would put an arm around each of their necks they would lift him into it. Before intrusting themselves so completely within his reach, Jack felt it prudent to remark with firmness, —

"Now, you mustn't try any tricks on us, Pete, for we're armed with knives and a gun, and plenty of cartridges. We wish to be friendly with you, if you'll let us; but, if you show any signs of treachery, we shall feel justified in throwing you overboard."

Jack was surprised at his ability to make so formidable an harangue to one who, in his normal condition, was more than a match for them both. As for Max, he felt at least two inches taller with pride on hearing his friend address the muscular, dangerous-looking half-breed in such downright style.

" Ya, ya," Pete assented assuringly.

Accordingly the boys carried him to the canoe in the fashion described, and laid him on his back. He seemed to be suffering considerably. Max, who sat in the stern facing Pete, took the precaution to place the rifle by his own side, though Pete was scarcely in a condition to carry out any evil designs. As soon as they started, it became apparent that the canoe had suffered considerably by her fall, in that the water began to trickle into her through sundry cracks imperceptible to the eye; but, by strenuous bailing, they were enabled to keep it from making serious progress, while, as regards comfort, the trio were as wet as could be already. The particulars of Pete's catastrophe were gleaned on the way by means of a few questions. His heavily laden canoe had struck a rock, and split in two; and the injury to his leg had been received at the same moment. He had never learned to swim, —a strange circumstance, which ·could be told equally of a large number of men whose livelihood is earned more or less upon the water.

It was about six o'clock as they came in sight of the Big Salmon Hole. No one appeared to be stirring, and Jack suggested that Max should fire the rifle in the air by way of announcing their arrival. A moment after the explosion, a number of heads were thrust out of the tents, and Bingo began to bark vehemently.

"It's Jack and Max come back," cried several voices, and the entire party came rushing down to the water's edge, with surprise written on their faces, which was doubly increased as they realized who was the stranger reclining in the canoe.

"Why, boys, what does this mean?" cried the

Colonel, seizing the nose of the canoe, and steadying it.

"Not very much," said Jack nonchalantly, as he stepped ashore. "Except one thing, — Max shot a bear."

"Shot a bear?"

"Really!"

"Hoorah!"

"Bully for you, Max! A bear! Max has killed a bear, Mr. Holt," cried Tom, completing the round of youthful exclamations that greeted Jack's announcement.

"Well done, Max," answered the Colonel gravely; "but that does not explain why you are both in this bedraggled condition, — and who is it with you?"

"Pete Labouisse, and I guess he has broken his leg," Jack answered laconically.

The half-breed had turned himself, and was surveying the party suspiciously from his dark eyes, and listening to every word.

"How did that happen?"

Jack looked at Max and laughed. Having given his word not to betray Pete, he felt it necessary to speak guardedly. "Running the Injun Falls. His canoe struck a rock, and got upset, and — and we followed him."

"Over the Indian Falls!" interrupted the Colonel.

"And are here alive to tell the tale!" exclaimed Mr. Holt, supplementing the Colonel's expression of horror.

"We really did," said Max, "and Jack saved Pete's life by jumping over after him."

The bewildered elders looked from one of the lads to the other, while a murmur of astonishment spread through the group. The soaked garments and generally exhausted appearance of the pair was eloquent testimony to the truth of their statement. Without asking further questions at the moment, the Colonel pulled up the canoe, and addressing Pete said, —

"You had better let us carry you up to the house, and see how much you're hurt."

The half-breed made no remonstrance to this proposal, recognizing doubtless that it was kindly meant, and that he was in no condition to resist his captors. Accordingly the Colonel and Mr. Holt, who smiled at thus turning the tables on his enemy, lifted the injured man, and carried him up to the cabin, followed by the six boys, whose tongues were becoming unloosened. Pete was laid on one of the bunks; and, after an examination, it plainly appeared that his leg was broken, and that he ought to be sent to the Basin at once. The suggestion of this plan seemed to alarm the victim excessively. He shook his head, and protested in vivid *patois*.

"But your leg must be set," said the Colonel. "If you stay here, inflammation will set in, and you'll die."

"Ya, ya," said Pete, indicating by the pantomime which accompanied this favorite ejaculation a preference to take the chances of never getting well, rather than go down to the village.

Jack and Max, who had been whispering together, now made signs to the Colonel and Mr. Holt to go out with them where they would be unobserved by the prisoner.

"We want you to promise something," said Jack, acting as the spokesman, "which is that Pete shall not be put in prison, or punished in any way."

"Why should he be punished?" asked the Colonel with a quizzical smile. "What has he done?"

"I didn't say he had done anything. But you will promise, won't you?"

"This is very mysterious. I don't know about passing such a sweeping act of indemnity. Eh, Mr. Schoolmaster?"

"It seems to me that as Pete has been punished pretty severely, we may safely do so, even to the extent of neglecting to wreak vengeance for the loss of the loon," answered Mr. Holt.

"Well, you hear what the Big Injun says, boys. I shall not stand in the way," answered the Colonel.

"That's first-rate," cried the petitioners.

"But now that the pardon is granted, you must let us into the secret," said the master.

Jack and Max saw no objection to this; and the salmon-spearing episode was unfolded with as much detail as the listeners would permit, in view of the fact that the two boys were still in wet clothing. Mr. Holt hurried them off as soon as possible to effect the necessary changes in their toilet, while Dubsy was making elaborate preparations for the relief of the inner man. The remaining boys clustered about the tent door, and put all sorts of questions regarding the exciting expedition. But it was not until the hungry heroes had broken their fast with something more palatable than half-cooked bear's meat, that their tongues wagged to the full satisfaction of themselves and everybody. It was difficult to say whether the killing of the bear or the passage over the falls aroused the more enthusiasm; and when Jack declared he would have been torn to pieces but' for Max's courage, Max called attention to the fact that Pete would certainly have been drowned had not Jack jumped overboard.

"All's well that ends well," said the Colonel presently. "You have each of you shown him-self a very plucky fellow, and I haven't the heart to indulge much in criticism, considering the results you have to show. But it is cer-tainly a wonder that either of you is here alive. And yet admitting that luck was on your side when you put yourselves in peril by attacking a bear with a single cartridge in the heart of the woods, and running falls that no boatman would run, you have the right, Max, to boast of a noble piece of daring when you risked your life to save your friend's, and you, Jack, of equal heroism when the instinct of humanity induced you to leap into the swift river to rescue one who had done you an injury. However rash, you are brave boys, and I am proud of you."

"And so is the Big Injun," added Mr. Holt. "When the Colonel praises, you may be sure that it is deserved, my dear fellows. And, apart from the courage displayed, I am glad to perceive that you have come back such excellent friends. I can see that all petty jealousies and mutual mistrust have vanished into respect and hearty liking for each other. Isn't that so? I don't need to ask, for I can discern it in your eyes."

"Whoever says anything against Max, will have me to reckon with after this," exclaimed Jack. "Though Max doesn't need assistance from any one, I can tell you that," he added significantly.

Max answered in a quiet tone, "I owe everything to you, Jack."

"Not more than I owe to you," was the stout answer.

"Each has received help from the other in the ways in which he needed it," said Mr. Holt, smiling contentedly.

The other boys, who had been awed into silence by the serious turn which the conversation had taken, were now delighted by the proposal which the Colonel made, that three cheers should be given for the heroes of the hour. These were vented with a will, and must have astonished Pete, who had been left to his own devices on the bunk after having been fortified by a hearty meal. Then Jack and Max, weary perhaps of answering questions, began to ask them, inquiring concerning the doings of the rest of the party during their absence. In reply they learned that the sport had been very satisfactory, thirty-nine salmon having been killed, and eleven lost. Dandy and Daisy were reported as having behaved themselves in a tractable manner, and were exhibited in sundry antics by Tom, who was devoting himself to their education. Nothing of great moment had occurred to vary the daily programme of angling and poling, under the influence of which healthy occupations one and all looked brown as berries.

At the first opportunity, Jack returned to the prisoner's bed-side, and explained to him that Colonel Russell had pledged his word that no mention should be made of what had happened at the Narrows; and by dint of assurances that Pete would be free to take his leave the moment he was well, and that he would be likely to lose his leg were he to remain where he was, the half-breed was induced to consent to the plan that he should be conveyed to the Basin. This accomplished, it became a question as to who should accompany Pete. Jack and Max were eager that some of the party should go up to the Narrows in order to recover possession of Bruin. After consideration it was agreed that Dubsy and Haseltine should escort the half-breed, and that the others should make a flying trip up river. Accordingly, as it was desirable to put Pete in a doctor's hands as soon as possible, the canoe was got ready at once, and before noon Dubsy and Hasy bade good-by to the Big Salmon Hole. After their departure, Jack and Max, who could scarcely keep their eyes open from fatigue and drowsiness, were thankful to creep under their mosquito-nettings, and go to sleep.

CHAPTER IX.

WHO WON THE RIFLE.

Two weeks more had passed, and camp was to be broken up for the last time on the morrow. The river was getting very low, and those salmon which had not gone far up to spawn were so logy that they would not even look at a fly. By most persistent efforts the Colonel had been able to capture but a single fish during the last four days, and in the same period no one else had taken any. The heat of midsummer was upon them, affecting the sportsmen, as well as the game, with a lack of energy. The total catch to date amounted to one hundred and seventeen salmon, averaging about twenty pounds, — in fact, a fraction over that figure, — so that there was naturally no incentive to remain longer from dissatisfaction at the score. The majority of the fish were safely buried in the ice-house. Those which had been killed at the

Narrows had been transported to the Big Salmon Hole, and there were others which had been left at camp No. 1. The boys were looking forward to sending home to their families and friends the finest specimens, and some had been " kippered " to serve as smoked salmon after the fishing season was over.

As a result of the second expedition to the Narrows, Bruin had been found after a somewhat protracted search. The bear's flesh was spoiled, but the skin had proved to be in fine condition; and the operation of skinning the creature, which the Colonel performed, had been watched with intense interest by Jack and Max and Joe, who were with him. Although the plan at first had been that all should visit the scene of the hand-to-hand encounter, the question suddenly presented itself as to what should be done with Dandy and Daisy. To lead them through the woods for so long a distance, was not to be thought of for a moment, especially as, owing to the fact that a canoe had to be carried up to take the place of the one in which the two boys had run the fall, all would be heavily burdened. Mr. Holt had suggested, as what seemed to him a happy solution of the difficulty, that the two pets should be allowed to go free; but the proposal was received with a round of horrified exclamations. As for Tom, he was very nearly moved to tears, and he had declared his preference to remain at home as a keeper rather than participate in the expedition on such distressing terms. Finally it had been arranged that Mr. Holt and he should accompany the others to the Narrows, and return to the youthful bears before night-fall. In this way they had been able to see the upper river and the famous cascade over which the two rash boys had come so near being swept to a watery grave. As the party stood together on the bank, and gazed at the sheet of water dashing down, there had been many expressions of amazement that the canoe had made the leap without disaster, and Jack and Max had fully realized for the first time their foolhardiness.

The party had returned to the Big Salmon Hole at the end of the fifth day without having met with any important adventures. No more bears had been seen, and the salmon at the Narrows had

not been in the humor for rising. They had taken
only a few. On their arrival they found Hasy
and Dubsy, who had been at camp for forty-eight
hours, and who reported that Pete, after a tranquil
trip down river, had been safely deposited by
them in the doctor's hands, without disclosures as
to the evil doings which had been the cause of his
injury. But, though close-mouthed as to the
passage of the Indian Falls, the two voyagers had
been unable to remain silent as to the killing of
the bear, an event which had caused the greatest
excitement in the little village.

On the part of those who had remained at
camp, Tom had to boast of the killing of a mink,
a weasel-like creature, which he had detected in
the act of eating a hole in a freshly caught salmon.
Tom had described the affair with great gusto to
the Colonel and the other boys on their return.

"I was sitting eating my luncheon, when I happened to glance in the direction of the fish, which
was lying under shelter of a shelving rock to
protect it from the sun; and there was a curious
creature, like a rat, only three or four times as
long, feasting on the salmon. I would have liked

to catch it alive, but I knew if I made any noise it would escape. I didn't even dare to call Mr. Holt, who was only a short distance off; but, after watching for a while, I reached out for the gun, and got a good aim. Then I fired, and the mink rolled over dead as Chelsea. But the salmon looked as if it had been bored out with an auger, and we threw it overboard."

Beyond this there had been nothing to chronicle. And now, on the following day, they were to start for home. All hands had been busy during the morning in building a large raft, on which the salmon and trout collected in the ice-house were to be fastened, and sent down to Gaspé Basin. Luncheon was finished, and the boys had arranged themselves in various comfortable postures to enjoy the balmy summer afternoon, the last that they were to pass in the woods. While they were thus sitting, the door of the cabin opened, and Mr. Holt and the Colonel, who had been closeted together since leaving the table, appeared. The Colonel carried in his hand the rifle which he had put up as a prize for the best sportsman. A hush of expectancy fell upon the group of boys. They felt that the interesting question, as to which of them should become its owner, was about to be settled.

The two seniors sat down on a rustic bench, and the Colonel laid the untarnished rifle on the table before him.

"Boys," said Mr. Holt. glancing pleasantly around the circle, "of course you all remember the handsome offer which Colonel Russell made you on the afternoon that we were approaching Gaspé. He and I have been talking the matter over since luncheon, for it seemed to us that the time had come for trying to arrive at a decision as to which of you is entitled to carry off the prize. But our task has proved by no means an easy one; and, after much consideration, we have finally decided to leave the matter to your own decision. We prefer that you boys should select by ballot the one among you who you think is most deserving of the rifle. Before I go on further, however," resumed the master, who had paused for a moment after making this announcement, "I wish to tell you all — and the Colonel has asked me to be his spokesman — that we are thoroughly pleased with your behavior during the weeks we have spent together. You have surpassed our expectations in showing yourselves manly, straightforward, good-natured fellows, and you have the right to be proud of your record as sportsmen. I don't mean that you have not done some foolish, rash, and silly things. You would scarcely be boys if you hadn't; but, on the whole, you have acquitted yourselves in such a manner that it is with sincere regret on our part that the time has come to part."

"Hear, hear!" interjected the Colonel.

"I feel pretty sure that you have had a pleasant vacation; and it is very easy to see, from the improved appearance of each one of you, that the life in the open air has done you good. We have had fine sport, and have been fortunate enough to escape mishaps. If you are not experienced salmon fishermen, you at least can land your fish in less time than five hours. Eh, Jack?"

A ripple of laughter ran around the circle at this sally.

"And now," continued Mr. Holt, "before you proceed to vote, I will make a few suggestions

for your guidance. I wish to remind you, in the
first place, that in most affairs of life opportunity
and chance are factors that have to be taken
into account. Of two men who start with equal
abilities, one may have the offer of a position
that brings into play his talents, and makes him
a name; while the other, with the same gifts,
remains obscure through lack of an occasion to
show what he can do. And yet, in estimating
these two men, one cannot withhold from him
who has done well his meed of praise because
the other might have deserved no less had the
opportunity been given him. Similarly, when
we came into the woods, you each had the same
chances of being put in positions which would
call forth your sportsmanlike qualities, and some
of you have been more fortunate in this respect
than others. It would surely not be fair that
the lucky ones should not have the benefit of
their luck. Then, again, while you ought certainly to take into account and give credit for
zealous effort to do well against disadvantages,
you should not forget the claims of natural aptitude. There is no reason that one who tries

hard should be ranked with one who tries hard and has proficiency at the same time. In like manner, though one may admire a little fellow for trying to do a big fellow's work, it is false sentiment to let pluck and ambition take the place of actual capacity. And now, if our plan strikes you favorably, and you have no questions to ask, you will each of you write on one of these pieces of paper the name of whomever you select; and I will collect them in my hat, and count them. The boy who has the most votes shall have the rifle."

For a moment, the boys exchanged half-amused, half-shy glances, then severally they came forward to receive from the master one of the slips in his hand. Thereupon each went a little apart by himself to think. Haseltine was the first to reach a conclusion.

"I've finished," he cried promptly; and folding his ballot he dropped it in the hat.

"So am I," said Dubsy. "Who wants my pencil?"

"Could a fellow vote for himself?" asked Tom humorously.

"Oh, yes, if he thought himself the best man!" answered the Colonel, who had stretched himself beneath a tree, and was watching the ceremony with interest.

"Well, I guess my modesty forbids," answered Tom; and writing a name on his piece of paper, he deposited it at the same time that Max and Joe presented theirs.

Jack was still standing pensively with the pencil between his lips. What name should he put down? His first thought had been to vote for Max; and then a voice had whispered that Max was his most formidable competitor, and that a vote for him was a vote against himself. Why not vote for Tom or Hasy? Both had done finely, and, moreover, Hasy was his particular friend.

"Come, Jack, we are waiting for you," said Mr. Holt, in a tone which almost betrayed knowledge of the struggle which was going on in the boy's mind. At its sound Jack started, realizing in an instant the meanness which he had been tempted to commit. With alacrity he wrote down in large letters "Max," and handed it to the master. Then came a few moments of suspense, while Mr. Holt, having emptied his hat upon the table, proceeded to scan the slips of paper. The Colonel sat placidly smoking.

"I'll bet one Jock Scott against three, that I can name the winner," exclaimed Haseltine; but the wager found no takers.

"It's exciting, isn't it?" said Max, who was leaning against a tree, close to Jack. His eyes were sparkling in proof of his assertion.

"Yes. I think you'll win. You ought to win. *I* voted for you."

"Thank you, Jack," Max said, in reply to the blunt, sturdy sentences. "So did I for you."

A rap on the table followed. Mr. Holt was ready to announce the result. "Whole number of ballots cast, six: Jack Hall, three; Max Fearing, three."

"A tie!" exclaimed the Colonel.

"A tie!" cried the rest, in appreciative echo.

"What are they to do?" asked Tom.

"We couldn't very well own it together," said Jack laughingly to Max. How happy he was that he had voted as he had! He could

not help reflecting that if he had won the rifle
by such a device he would have felt like casting
it into the sea.

"We might toss up for it," said Dubsy.

Jack shook his head. Leaving so serious a
matter to chance did not suit him.

"We ought to have provided for such a con-
tingency," said Mr. Holt. "As Jack says, though,
you can't very well own it together."

"I have an idea," said the Colonel, who had
been puffing reflectively. "Suppose you shoot
for it."

"With the rifle?" cried Jack.

"Ay, ay."

"A capital plan," said Mr. Holt. "Neither of
the two has any advantage in point of experience.
How does it strike you, boys?"

The victorious pair looked at each other. "I'm
willing if you are, Max."

"It seems as fair a way as any."

The others approved highly of the scheme, and
after a short debate the following arrangements
were made: A target a foot square, consisting
of a piece of clean wood marked with a bull's-

eye and another alternate black ring, was fastened against a tree about twenty-five yards distant. Each of the competitors was to have three shots; and the one who hit the center, or came nearest to it, was to take the prize. No shot beyond the outer black ring was to count; and in case neither of the marksmen succeeded in planting a bullet inside of this, three more shots were to be fired by each.

"It's a match between two cock-shots," said Hasy, who, having had some practice in shooting in the past, was pleased to jibe. "As you couldn't hit a bear at a yard, Jack, you're not likely to be able to hit a bit of wood at twenty-five."

"I did hit the bear," was the answer.

"He didn't seem to mind it, though," exclaimed Tom, taking his turn at chaffing. "I think, Colonel Russell, that a barn-door would be the most sensible thing for them to fire at. We may not get away for a week, if we have to stay until Jack or Max hits that bull's-eye."

"You should have spoken sooner," said the Colonel, who had been busy marking the target

by means of some blacking and some soot from
the fire-place. "This is just ready."

Although neither of the contestants had ever
practiced with a rifle before this summer, each
of them had acquired more or less proficiency
in shooting at objects during the past few weeks,
so that they were not entirely novices. They
were to fire alternately, and the choice of shooting first or last fell to Jack. He decided to
have Max begin.

The Colonel loaded the new rifle deliberately,
and placed it in Max's hands. There was a hush
of intense excitement as he raised it to his
shoulder and took aim. Although each of the
boys, in voting, had been able to arrive at a
choice, there was not one of them who was not
glad to see the matter settled in this way. Joe
had voted for his brother, but he had been conscious that Jack had serious claims on the prize;
and similarly Dubsy and Haseltine, though faithful to their friend, could not deny that Max was
a close second. Tom, too, had finally selected
the slayer of Bruin in preference to Pete's rescuer
only after grave hesitation.

There came a sharp report, and immediately the whole party dashed forward to inspect the result of Max's first shot. A score of eyes were riveted on the target, but not one of them could discern a trace of the rifle-ball.

"Cracky! He hasn't even hit the tree," cried Haseltine, convulsed with mirth.

So it certainly appeared. Neither the rings nor the bark of the pine trunk were scarred. There was much merriment, and poor Max blushed vividly.

"You were too nervous. You'll do better next time," said Mr. Holt kindly.

All retraced their steps, and it was now Jack's turn. He reflected that he could not do worse than Max, but he felt by no means confident of being able to succeed better. However, he put on a determined front. He would not, if possible, be thwarted by nervousness. So he received the freshly loaded rifle with studied calm, and began to scrutinize the glittering barrel and the adroit breech-loading action.

"Is it allowable to fire sitting?" he asked the Colonel.

"Yes. You may sit down or lie down, and you

may rest the rifle in any way you choose, provided you rest it against some part of the body."

"Oh!" said Jack, as though he regarded this sanction as a boon; and consequently he proceeded to test the advantages of various squatting and recumbent postures. He even tried supporting the muzzle upon his crossed knees, after the manner of the methods of noted marksmen concerning which he had read. But somehow none of these experiments inspired him with confidence. By the time he had risen to his feet again, he had decided to aim in the ordinary way, which he did with precision.

"Bang!"

Away flew the reconnoiterers; and again there was blank staring at the target, which made Jack feel decidedly uneasy. He was straining his own eyes to discover a bullet-hole, but in vain. Another shout of derision was uttered by Hasy. He had missed, too, after all this preparation.

"No advantage on either side so far," said the Colonel with a laugh. Both of the contestants looked decidedly sheepish; and Max, as he raised the rifle for the second time, was the victim of numerous guying remarks, which Mr. Holt checked by a considerate "Hush! You may unsteady his aim."

"It couldn't be worse than it is," said Tom, below his breath.

Nevertheless, there was dead silence before Max pulled the trigger.

A moment later Hasy, who had darted ahead and was examining the mark, cried eagerly, —

"He has hit it."

Such was the case. There were the evident marks of a ball in the middle of the white ring next to the bull's-eye.

"Not a bad shot, by any means," said the Colonel. "You'll have to shoot well to improve on it, Jack," he added.

"I fear that my goose is cooked," replied our hero a little despondently.

"Nonsense," said Mr. Holt. "That doesn't sound like you, Jack."

"It doesn't mean I'm not going to try hard all the same," was the answer.

"That's the right spirit," said Colonel Russell pleasantly.

Crack went the rifle again.

"I saw the wood fly," cried Dubsy.

"Hurrah!" The cheer gladdened Jack's heart as he reached the tree.

"You've hit it. Same ring, but a little nearer," exclaimed several voices together.

"So I have," said Jack, as he scanned the target. The ball had struck in the white on the opposite side to Max's, and, though there was very little difference between them, it was plainly the nearer of the two to the center.

"Good enough, Jack," said Max. "I can't beat that."

"I'm afraid you will, though."

There were no more remarks about cock-shots. Ridicule had changed to absorbed attention, as Max took his position for his final shot.

"I think I missed," he said, as the report echoed through the hills.

"Bull's-eye!"

"Is it, though? Which is it? Hurrah!"

"Is it on the line? Hard to tell, though. Mighty close."

"Just on the line, I should say."

The last exclamation came from the Colonel, and, as was apt to be the case, was decisive. Careful scrutiny showed that the ball had penetrated the line, dividing the center from the inner circle. But, though not a plump bull's-eye shot, it was an improvement on any of the others, and could be beaten only by one.

"What did I tell you, Max?" said Jack.

"I was lucky."

Despite this modest assertion, Max could not help looking pleased, though he showed no undue signs of elation; and it was pardonable that poor Jack, who had set his heart on winning, should feel a trifle galled. He resolutely bit his lip, which was quivering despite his every wish to seem cool and indifferent, and stalked silently back to the spot from which he was to fire. But, though well aware that the chances of victory were very much against him, he took the rifle in hand with the fixed purpose to strain every nerve to win. There was an impressive stillness as he aimed, and to those who were watching it seemed as though the report would never come.

After firing, he stood still and let the others run forward. He did not care to look. He had waited before pulling the trigger until he had covered the black spot precisely, and he felt that he could do no more.

" Hurrah — Jack — Jack — bull's-eye — you've hit the bull's-eye — 'rah, 'rah, 'rah — bull's-eye — first-rate — right in the center." A babel of voices rang in his ears, and in another instant Hasy and Dubsy were shaking his hands as though they would pull them off.

" You've won. You've hit the bull's-eye plump in the middle," one of them exclaimed, in answer to his wondering expression.

There could be no doubt of it now. The Colonel was advancing to meet him with out-stretched hand.

" Well done, well done, Jack. The odds against you were enough to unsteady a practiced eye, and you have won grandly."

Half laughing, half crying with excitement, he made his way to the target to see with his own eyes what he had done. Max was still smiling, and his congratulatory grip was the heartiest of

all, though one could see he was badly disappointed, as was to be expected.

"Well, you deserve the rifle, anyway, Jack,"
he was generous enough to say. "You're naturally a sportsman, and I'm only a manufactured
one. What Mr. Holt said about natural aptitude
was perfectly true."

Jack was too bewildered and excited at the
moment to dispute the point, but his glad look
assured Max of his gratitude. He put his finger
into the bullet-hole. As they had told him, the
ball had hit exactly in the center of the bull's-
eye.

"The rifle is your property now," said the
Colonel. "It is a good one, I assure you."

"I'll shoot you a match for it, — best three
shots in five," exclaimed Haseltine jauntily.

The victor laughed, and shook his head.

"Jack is willing to let well enough alone," said
the master, "and you can hardly blame him. With
due respect to his skill, he would not be likely
to duplicate that last shot in a hurry."

It is not agreeable to bid farewell to a pleasant
scene. Although, owing to the long absence from

civilization, all felt that soft beds and home cookery, and even brick sidewalks, would not be uncongenial, there was no one of the party on the following day who did not feel regret to see the picturesque banks slip away on either side, as the canoes glided swiftly down to Gaspé Basin. The raft was sent ahead soon after breakfast, and they followed shortly. It was all downhill work, so to speak, and the miles made sport of the hours. It seemed but a very brief time before camp No. 1 was reached, where a landing was made to take a last glimpse at the familiar sights. Perfect quiet reigned over the neighborhood of the little cabin, and there were no evidences that the mother bear had returned in search of her young. A few fish which had been left in the ice-house were taken on board, and then the paddles were resumed, and the canoes sped again on their way. The fall in the river since they had ascended it was very noticeable. There were bare patches of stones where then there had been a swift rapid. In some places the middle of the bed was quite bare, and the water flowed in a narrow channel on either side. Twice the raft was discovered aground and sent on its way.

At last there were no more rapids; the river widened and became stiller, and the nets were reached. The first house and the first horse excited interest, and presently their nostrils caught the savor of the sea. The air felt cooler, too, so that those who were not paddling were glad to put on their jackets. Their approach had been heralded by the salmon, so that Annette was at his landing waiting.

It was pleasant to the boys to stretch their cramped limbs in a good run up the bank, and across the fields green with the bounty of summer. It did not take George Coffin long to learn of their arrival, and to put in an appearance with the trotter and his other team to take their belongings down to the "Admiral," which was to sail that evening, as they knew. And with him came old William, one vast grin of pleasure, and the stalwart Jimmy, eager to hear and see the results of the expedition. Much of the news had been gleaned from Pete's escort, so that congratulations were in order.

"And so you killed a bear, after all!" said William to Jack.

"It was Max who killed him. I tried to, but I didn't succeed."

"I know, I know. I heard all about it," said the old guide, nodding delightedly.

"There's something, though, you haven't heard," said the Colonel, "which is that these two same young scapegraces took it into their heads to run the Indian Falls."

"The Injun Falls! I guess not," exclaimed Jimmy. "That's too tall a story even for us to swallow, Colonel."

"They did it, though," said Mr. Holt; "and, as I've repeated to them many times already, it's a wonder they're alive to tell the tale."

"That's gospel truth," said Jimmy. "Run them Injun Falls! And you broke nothing?"

"We took in lots of water," answered Jack.

"And she leaked afterwards," said Max.

"Yes, I guess she did," said the Colonel with a laugh.

"You boys can't be beat," said old William,

who, dazed by the astounding statement, had been unable to utter a word.

"But what made you run 'em?" asked Jimmy, still aghast.

"Oh, we thought we would!" said Jack coolly. "You told me once you thought they could be run."

The guides, whatever their suspicions, had to be satisfied with this explanation. Dubsy and Hasy, at the time they brought down the half-breed, had obeyed instructions by stating simply that he had been saved from drowning in one of the rapids by Jack; and, though questioned adroitly, they had managed not to betray their prisoner. It was Hasy who now turned the conversation by inquiring, —

"How's Pete?"

"He's mending fast," said George. "I see him sitting at his shanty door sunning himself yesterday, and he wanted to know when I expected you down river."

"He might have never come down himself, and there'd have been mighty little mourning," said Jimmy, in which caustic sentiment he was

supported by a growl from his father, that spoke
volumes.

There was no time for further conversation at
the moment, as the traps had to be stowed in the
cart, and preparations made for departure; but
when the white horse had begun to trot, the ears
of George were delighted with abundant details
concerning the summer school, which were
repeated and supplemented when they were all
gathered around Mrs. Dumaresque's ample hearth
after supper. The guides were fairly entranced
by the description of the encounter with Bruin,
and the wonderful passage of the falls, the
occasion of which was kept shrouded in mystery
to the end. Pete was seen, and cheered by a
present of money, in return for which he gave
assurance that seemed genuine of a wish to
renounce salmon-spearing, and set up as an
honest cobbler. The guides boxed up for trans-
portation, in quantities of snow-ice, a number of
the largest fish; and Dandy and Daisy, having
been the recipients of much admiration, were
safely convoyed on board ship in advance of their
owners, who lingered to the last, loath to leave

such pleasant scenes. But all things delightful must have their end; and the whistle of the "Admiral" warned the still prattling boys, who had not half exhausted their adventures, that the hour for departure was at hand. The leave-taking was genuinely regretful on either side; and when the wharf was reached, old Joe Eden, to whom a fine salmon had been sent, was there to wish them a prosperous voyage, and to express the general hope of the village, that they would all return another summer. The second whistle cut short his eloquence, and the Colonel turning to George asked, —

"Are the fish aboard?"

"Everything, Colonel. Fish, rods, bags, — nothing left behind."

"Well, time we were off."

But Mr. Eden detained him by the button. "Great story that they're telling down at Campbellton about one of your young gentlemen."

"What story is that, Joe?"

"Why, they say he was twenty-four hours landing that fish, and that he had three square meals over him."

"Do you hear that, Jack Hall?" cried the Colonel, as he burst into a peal of laughter, in which every one joined; and before the merriment had subsided, they were crossing the gang-plank of the "Admiral."

"Good-by, Colonel Russell.   Good-by, Mr. Holt. Good-by, boys."

"Good-by, George, good-by."

"Good-by, William."

"Good-by, Jimmy."

Joe Eden, too, and many others are shouting and waving. The smoke-stack puffs vigorously, sending out a train of fiery cinders. The voices grow fainter, the figures fade into the night, and the summer school is steaming away from Gaspé Basin.